RIDE, REBELS!

RIDE, REBELS!

Adventures of the Iron Scouts

MANLY WADE WELLMAN

IVES WASHBURN, INC.

NEW YORK

Wellman, Manly Wade, 1905– Ride, rebels! Adventures of the
Iron Scouts. New York, I. Washburn [1959] 180 p. illus.
21 cm. 1. U. S.—Hist.—Civil War—Fiction. I. Title.
PZ7.W458Ri 813.54 59–9371 ‡ Library of Congress

SECOND PRINTING, JULY 1960
OCLC # 1498316

MANUFACTURED IN THE UNITED STATES OF AMERICA

When you rise to the sound of the bugles
With your comrades on Judgment Day,
Just let it be said, "There's an old Confed.,
And he's wearing the same old gray. . . ."

Contents

RIDE, REBELS!

❧ 1 ❦

Raiders and Scouts

It was over in the mild winter twilight before it had really begun—half a company of mounted bluecoats pouncing on two squads of gray-clad cavalry lounging by the riverside, like a skyful of hawks grabbing a lesser number of sparrows.

Out of the leafless thickets and brush those Federal troopers had burst, at full gallop, from both directions on the riverbank and from below the ford. So complete was the surprise that the Confederates could not fire a shot. Melancholy, helpless, every man of that picket was rounded up and made prisoner.

From a scant hundred yards' distance, two other men in blue knelt beside their horses in evergreen scrub and watched helplessly.

"One minute more," muttered young Clay Buckner, "and we'd have been there too, captured by Yankees."

"It's not too late to plug one," growled his companion, lifting his long-barreled rifle to take aim at the officer commanding the Union cavalry.

"No, Bob!" Clay sprang up and knocked the rifle

3

muzzle aside, then snatched the weapon away. "Don't be a fool, Bob Dulin, they'd shoot back at us—"

"I'm not scared of bullets," Bob Dulin snarled, trying to grab his rifle again. "Do you think I'm in the Iron Scouts to play pattycake?"

"You're in the Iron Scouts to find out what the Yanks are up to," Clay snapped.

"Yanks killed my brother Lem," said Bob Dulin. He was no older than Clay, and not so large, but his dark hair and darker fury made him seem older. "They killed my little brother Willie, and John died of camp fever. I'm the last Dulin left, and I'm going to score one hundred blue-coated thieves—"

"Not just now," interrupted Clay. "Get back yonder and tell Shadburne and the rest of the boys what happened here—that we saw a hard-riding bunch of Union cavalry capture the picket at Ely's Ford and open it wide for more Yankees to cross!"

"Who are you ordering to carry messages?" complained Bob Dulin, but he turned, put foot in stirrup, and mounted his horse. "Give me back my shooting iron, Clay."

Clay handed him the rifle. Dulin clucked to his horse and rode back along the riverbank, away from the ford. Alone, Clay watched while the disarmed Confederates were led back across the river under alert guard.

Clay shook his brown-shocked head. The picket surprised, the ford captured—Yankees were on the move, this February 29 in 1864, this extra day of grief in a grievous year for the defenders of the Rapidan River in Virginia. He, Clay Buckner, was just a few days short of his nineteenth birthday and of the end of his first year of Confederate military service. Briefly he remembered March of 1863, his ride from his North Carolina home to join Jeb Stuart's cavalry, how he had become one of the Iron Scouts, who prowled the flanks and rear of the great stubborn Federal army that couldn't seem to learn it wasn't wanted in Virginia. . . .

More horsemen splashed across and into view in the dusk. Clay patted his own horse, brown, swift Cherokee, and softly commanded him to stand; then he crept forward on hands and knees to where he could see better. As the Federals reached the south bank, they made a column of fours. One formation rode away, more than twenty sets of fours—say, a hundred men. A second unit completed itself and followed. Another did likewise.

"Clay."

That soft Texas voice was Sergeant George Shadburne's, chief of the Iron Scouts. His tussock of beard looked black in the deepening gloom behind Clay's shoulder. "How many?" he asked.

"Three hundred so far," reported Clay. "Here's another hundred, starting south on the road."

They watched together. "And a fifth hundred," said Shadburne tensely, "heading for Spottsylvania. That's on the road to Richmond. Only five hundred men— wait, look. An officer's leaving two men here by the ford."

Shadburne scrambled cautiously through the brush.

Clay followed. Very close to the ford, they strained their eyes to see through the deepening darkness. The last of the five hundred riders had taken the road. Only the two men remained.

"A guard," whispered Clay, but Shadburne shook his head until his bushy whiskers stirred a breeze.

"No, they'd leave more men than that for a guard. That pair is just to report to a bigger force that will follow."

Shadburne turned and hurried back, almost running on all fours like a prowling animal of the night. Clay crouched and followed his sergeant. They caught the bridles of their waiting horses, rose erect, and hurried still farther to where three other men stood by their own mounts: Dulin, of course, and young Hugh Scott, and Jud Prioleau with his black spike of chin beard.

Quickly Shadburne described what he and Clay had seen. Then: "Mount," he ordered. "We'll slip in and grab those two Yankees at the ford."

"Let me go in first," growled Dulin.

"I said grab them, not shoot them." Shadburne peered at his companions, one after another. "We all have blue Federal overcoats, we can pass in the dark for their friends. Clay Buckner, you and Hugh Scott are wearing Yankee pants and boots. Ride at the head. Now, we'll circle south and come up the road to the ford. We're a party returning from that advance force, understand? And we're carrying messages back to the main body that must be following."

Shadburne led them away in a great curving approach to the road below the ford. As they came near, he halted them and sent Prioleau forward on foot to make sure that the raiders had passed southward. Then he spoke a last word:

"Buckner and Scott, you ride in front. You have good blue uniforms and you look young and honest—no beards. They'll trust you. I'll come behind you, and I'll do any talking that has to be done. Dulin and Prioleau, follow me closely. When I say the word, grab them."

They emerged upon the road. Moonlight made the hard-tramped earth white as they trotted riverward.

"Halt!" came a challenge from ahead. "Who goes there?"

"Quiet down," called back Shadburne. "Do you want the rebels to hear us?"

They rode toward the two horsemen by the water. Clay saw pistols gleaming in the lifted hands of the Federals.

"Quiet," said Shadburne again. "We're from the advance. The woods are full of rebels—they haven't discovered our move yet, but—"

"Who are you?" demanded one of the two by the ford, leaning past his horse's neck to peer at Clay. "Give the countersign."

"No time for that," said Shadburne impatiently, and urged his horse past Clay toward the nearest Federal. "You can't tell who might be listening to our countersigns. We're going to warn the others."

"We can't be that bad off," said the other Union trooper as Clay came up on his other side.

"You're worse off than that," Shadburne told the two. "You're our prisoners."

He caught the gun hand of the man nearest him and leveled his own big dragoon revolver. At the same moment Clay reined Cherokee close against the other man's horse and shoved his pistol muzzle against the blue-jacketed ribs.

"Not a word or move," warned Clay.

Dulin and Prioleau pressed in from beyond, weapons in hand. Clay and Shadburne disarmed their captives.

"Get down, you Yankees," ordered Shadburne, and he himself jumped from his saddle. "We don't want to hurt you, but we mean business. Now, what's going on here?"

"If you're so clever, you can figure it out yourself," growled the bigger of the two prisoners.

Clay rummaged a saddlebag carried by the horse beside him. "Rations in here," he reported. "Hard crackers—ten, a dozen—and some coffee and salt. Looks like three days' rations, but no meat."

"They figure to capture meat on the way to Richmond," guessed Shadburne. "Three days' bread and coffee means a raid deep down yonder. All right, one of you, tell me how many are in the next party?"

"What makes you think there's a next party?" said the smaller Federal.

"Buckner, Scott," snapped out Shadburne, "get on the horses of these two men. You'll act as the videttes at this ford. Find out all you can about the main body.

Prioleau and Dulin, take these prisoners to our head-quarters."

The men moved to obey.

"I'll ride your horse, Clay," said Shadburne. "My old nag's tired, and I'll put a prisoner on him. Nobody will escape very far on my horse tonight."

"Just let either of them try to escape!" put in Dulin fiercely.

Clay and Hugh Scott mounted the captured horses, Dulin and Prioleau escorted the two captured blue-coats away. Shadburne lingered a moment by the ford.

"This new bunch will be big, if it has an advance guard of five hundred," he said. "Be dead sure what the main body's up to, then cut east and head for General Hampton's headquarters. He's at Milford—fifteen, eighteen miles away. Tell him what you know, but make certain you know it before you ride off."

He brought Cherokee around and started south.

"Where are you going?" called Hugh Scott.

"After the advance guard," came back Shadburne's reply as he rode away in the moonlight.

Sitting their captured horses, Clay and Hugh felt as if half a regiment of stout allies had deserted them. They gazed at each other silently.

In many ways the two boys were alike. Hugh Scott, the South Carolinian, had just passed his nineteenth birthday; Clay Buckner was a few days short of his, but he was taller and stronger-made than his companion. On the other hand, Clay had but a single year of Iron

Scouts service, while Scott had ridden with Shadburne and the Ghost Battalion since early in 1862. He had spent more weeks behind Federal lines than in front of them.

Scott holstered his revolver and explored a saddle-bag. Digging out a hardtack, he bit into it. Neither youngster had eaten since noon, and just now it seemed that a hard and dangerous night's work lay before them.

"What's the time?" asked Hugh between mouthfuls, and Clay produced a silver watch.

"Nearly nine," he said. "Those other Yankees—"

"Hark!" interrupted Hugh. "I hear them."

From far away a muffled clatter of metal sounded—saber sheaths or bridle fastenings.

"Too many to fight," nodded Clay, "so let's outthink them. Just us two against an army, but they don't know we're rebels."

The noise grew loud and clear. Men rode toward them. Trees shaded the road across the stream. The foremost of the riders reined in his horse, fetlock deep in the water, and rose in his stirrups, peering.

"Come across, it's all right," Clay invited him.

Half a dozen rode across at a splashing trot. Clay saluted the officer who led them. "Advance party's gone a good hour, sir," he reported crisply.

"And no trouble?" prompted the officer.

"Not a whisper."

The officer rode on. More men followed, and Clay silently counted and computed. A company of a hundred crossed, formed anew, and moved on. Another, another, and another poured across.

A group of officers crossed together and reined to the side of the road while other companies made the journey from bank to bank. The moonlight outlined for Clay a lean rider on a splendid dark horse, a fox-faced young man with bushy side whiskers and gold-braided sleeves.

"The map, Major," said the fox-faced one in a flat, nasal voice, and someone spread a paper across his saddle horn for him. A long finger slid along the paper. "Twelve miles to Spottsylvania, is it? We'll be there by midnight—our advance will, anyway. Is the advance all right?"

"These men say it is, General," said an officer, and the general turned his whiskered young face toward them.

"Are you the ford detail?"

"Yes, sir," said Clay, as confidently as he could manage.

"How far ahead of us did the advance cross?"

"About an hour, General."

"Good." The general swerved his big horse and glanced up at the moon. "Beautiful night, gentlemen! That moon will guide us nearly to Richmond. I'll double my five-thousand-dollar bet that we're there by sundown tomorrow."

"No takers, General Kilpatrick," said one of the officers, laughing.

Kilpatrick? Then this was Judson Kilpatrick, the headlong young brigadier who, Yankees thought, was a sort of Northern Jeb Stuart. Kilpatrick had fought hard at Gettysburg, remembered Clay. Now he was going to Richmond, to fight hard again.

The general and his officers and couriers rode on. More companies followed. Ten made a regiment, ten more made another regiment. Four regiments in all, Clay figured—forty companies of nearly a hundred men each, nearly four thousand men—when the last reached the south side of Ely's Ford. They clattered away on that road toward Spottsylvania in the light of the bright moon that General Kilpatrick had so admired.

"Now," said Hugh Scott, as the hoofs became duller in their thunder.

He and Clay rode swiftly eastward along another road, little more than a trail, toward the headquarters of General Wade Hampton's division of the Confederate Army.

≫ 2 ≪
Pursuit

General Hampton's headquarters were at a tall, shabby old house, surrounded by tents and rickety huts. As Hugh and Clay rode in, a sentry hailed them with a cry for the password.

"Hush your fuss, we're Iron Scouts!" snapped out Hugh.

"All I see is your Yankee uniforms," yelled back the sentry. "Halt where you are! Corporal of the guard, Post Number Four!"

A corporal came running. "Yankees, you say?" he demanded. "Oh, hello, Scott. Hello, Buckner. Let them past, sentry, they're all right."

They dismounted on the splintered porch of the headquarters building. Young Lieutenant Preston Hampton, the general's tall, tawny son, met them at the door.

"Enemy raiders," reported Clay at once. "We must see the general."

"Raiders?" That was Major Barker, assistant adjutant general for the division. "How many?"

"More than four thousand," said Scott. "Five hundred in the advance party, the rest in a single body—guns and horses, with General Kilpatrick in command."

"They swallowed our picket at Ely's Ford," added Clay, "and they're off to Spottsylvania."

Preston Hampton had hurried to an inner room. Now he returned.

"The general will be here at once," he said. Then to Barker: "He wants to know how many men can ride at once."

Barker shook his head dolefully. "Not many. General Stuart took the rest of the Cavalry Corp west, on report of Yankee movements there. Most of our division is spread thin, on picket duty here and there—"

In strode a giant figure, buttoning a gray tunic under a dark-bearded chin. It was General Wade Hampton of South Carolina. In the candlelight he looked seven feet tall and five feet wide.

"Hello, Scott," he said. "That's Buckner with you, isn't it? Now, what's this rumor about a raid?"

"It's no rumor, General," Clay assured him, and told what he and the others had seen and surmised. The big general tugged a fistful of his beard.

"That's how an army can act with twice the cavalry of its opponent," he rumbled. "That Yankee movement over toward Charlottesville, where General Stuart hurried yesterday—it was a blind. This Richmond attempt is the real stroke. Barker, how many can we get into the saddle?"

"Two or three hundred, General," replied Barker, shuffling papers at a desk. "Not enough—"

"They'll have to be enough," broke in Hampton. "Wake them up and get them ready! Two days' rations to each man, of whatever we have on hand! As soon as they're mounted, we'll leave."

Barker and Preston Hampton raced out and away. The general looked from one young scout to the other.

"Rations," he said again. "This command has nothing worthy of the name. A little bacon, some corn meal, no coffee."

"Pardon me, General," ventured Hugh Scott. "We captured horses, and there was some stuff in the saddlebags."

He held out a small cloth sack. Hampton took it, untied the mouth, and held it to his bearded face. He sniffed loudly.

"Coffee!" he cried. "Nectar of the gods!" He took a long stride to a door at the left of the hall, and rapped resoundingly with the big fist that held the bag.

"Kit!" he shouted. "Kit Goodwyn, are you awake?"

The door opened, and out peered a dark face. "Been awake ever since those scouts come in, General."

"Here's some real coffee," said General Hampton. "Have you water boiling on the stove in there? Hurry up and bring three mugs of coffee."

He tossed the sack. A brown hand flashed up to catch it.

"And a fourth mug for yourself, Kit," added the general.

"Yes, *sir!*"

Kit Goodwyn vanished into his quarters. "Sit down,

you two," bade Hampton, tramped back to his room, then emerged buckling a belt from which hung his huge saber and a holstered pistol. Over his brawny arm he carried a gray cloak, and he held a broad hat with a palmetto badge looping up its brim. Kit Goodwyn came in with three steaming tin mugs. Gratefully Clay and Hugh sipped strong hot coffee with their general. As they finished, Major Barker reappeared.

"We woke up every man present with the First and Second North Carolina," he said, saluting. "Three hundred and four officers and men. Their commissaries are issuing bacon and cold corn pone."

"Colonel Bradley Johnson may have a few of his Marylanders in camp east of here," suggested Hampton. "Send a courier to tell him to follow with whatever he can bring. Kit! Package up some food for me." He looked at Clay. "Are you and Scott well mounted?"

"Those Federal horses are good ones," replied Clay.

"Old-style horse thieves used to say that a stolen horse carries you well," nodded Hampton. "All right, you and Scott ride with me at the head of the column. We'll strike toward Richmond; I want to catch up with those Yankees as soon as possible." Clay saw the general's heavy beard stir like wind-swept foliage as the square jaw set itself. "Find them and fight them. Come on."

They went out into the night together, the huge general, his adjutant, and the two scouts. An orderly led up a gigantic bay charger. That was Butler, Clay knew, Hampton's war horse. Lightly as a featherweight, the

big man swung into the saddle. Clay, Hugh, and Major
Barker mounted their own ready animals and followed
Hampton through the moonlight toward where a dark
throng of horsemen waited, four behind four.

"Bring them along, Colonel," said Hampton to the
officer in front. "Here, Buckner, do you know these
roads?"

"I was over them during the Chancellorsville campaign last year, General."

"We're going due south. You and Scott go ahead and
look for the enemy. We'll be just behind you, ready for
anything you find."

Hugh and Clay cantered off in advance of the troops.

"Did you notice, Clay?" asked Hugh. "Our main
body's about three hundred strong. Smaller than that
advance party of theirs."

"We're all advance party," replied Clay.

"No, you and I are the advance party. Two rebels
on stolen horses, neither of us old enough to raise chin
whiskers. We're the advance party."

"All right, let's keep advancing along this road."

A rider clattered toward them. At once Hugh and
Clay pulled their horses to right and left, stopping at
the sides of the road. Pistols ready in their hands, they
waited as the rider loped toward them.

"Halt!" challenged Clay, and the rider pulled up.
"Don't draw a weapon," Clay warned. Then: "Hey, it's
Shadburne!"

"Yes, you two heroes," growled the sergeant. "What
are you up to in these parts?"

"Showing the way to Big Wade and three hundred North Carolinians." Clay informed him. "We're out to whip those four thousand Yankees that headed down to Richmond."

"Wade Hampton's behind you? Good, because I found more. The Yankee advance headed due south at Spottsylvania. The rest of it, that big main bunch, slid off southeast toward Richmond."

Hoofs sounded behind them. Wade Hampton reined in his mighty horse beside the scouts. "That sounds like Shadburne's voice," he said.

"Yes, General Hampton. The raiders divided their forces. Part of them headed south, the others slanted toward Richmond."

"That means they'll try to attack above and below," said Hampton quickly. "Well, let's follow the larger force. Stay with me, Shadburne. You other scouts, keep on ahead."

"One moment, Sergeant," interposed Clay. "You're riding my horse."

"So I am. Let's trade."

In a trice they had swapped mounts. Cherokee whinnied gently as his master picked up the bridle. Clay and Hugh rode forward again.

"Clay," said Hugh after some moments, "when you gave Shadburne that Yankee horse you gave him two saddlebags full of hardtack."

"That's true," Clay half-wailed, "and all the coffee we had left."

They rode into the morning, and with the morning

came clouds and rain, then cold, cold winds that changed the rain into sleet. The hard icy crystals drove like tiny arrows into Clay's face, rattled on the dirt road like pebbles. Clay twitched up the collar of his Yankee blue overcoat, dragged down his slouch hat, and drew captured woolen gloves on to his hands. He patted Cherokee's shoulder and told him to be brave as they moved ahead on the way to Richmond and combat, along the road between stretches of woods, naked fields, yards with big and small houses.

It was past ten o'clock when they splashed across a small stream that was beginning to freeze over. The sleet powdered their hats and coats and the brown hides of their horses.

A courier overtook them there, telling them to halt. Peering backward through the storm, Clay saw more riders approaching. Shadburne lifted an arm in greeting. The big man on the big horse would be General Hampton. The general's tall young son rode with the party, and a couple of officers, and—yes, Bob Dulin and Jud Prioleau, also in blue Federal overcoats.

"We'll rest an hour," said Hampton. "Kilpatrick will have to rest his horses for longer than that if he intends to be able to charge outside Richmond. And he left Ely's Ford at midnight, long before we left Milford, but Milford's much closer to Richmond. Somewhere along the way we'll catch up with him."

Clay was already off Cherokee, leading him under the shelter of pine branches. He loosened the saddle girth, and found the woolen cloth he kept to rub him with. Hampton nodded in approval as he watched Clay care for his horse, then reined around and walked his own huge charger toward the men behind. Shadburne, also dismounted, kicked together some wood, broke dry twigs from the pine that sheltered Cherokee, and knelt to kindle a fire.

"Give my horse a rub when you're through with yours," he told Clay, "and I'll heat this canful of water and make us all some coffee."

"So you found Clay's coffee," accused Hugh, busy with his own mount.

"Shucks, that's the first thing I looked for when we swapped horses," replied Shadburne, teeth gleaming in his brown beard.

He trotted to the little stream and came back with water in the can. He balanced this on rocks above the fire. Carefully he fed larger chunks of wood into the blaze. Dulin and Prioleau led up their horses and thankfully accepted some of the coffee. Shadburne and Scott distributed big hardtacks, and Dulin produced a lump of boiled smoked pork, which he sliced wth a deadly-looking clasp knife.

The hour was up as they finished eating, and on they rode again. The advance patrol of Iron Scouts was re-enforced by comrades, experienced trailers and enemy watchers—Jim Sloan, who was from North Carolina like Clay; Barney Hennegan, an even bigger man than General Hampton but furtive and cunning as a mink for all his size; Dick Hogan, who was Shadburne's fellow sergeant; Jack Shoolbred with his tuft of chin beard; Shake Harris, who disliked being reminded that he had been christened William Shakespeare; black-haired, black-eyed Bill Mikler. Shadburne directed the eleven of them, spreading them through the country to scout from ridges and hilltops for a glimpse of blue cavalry through the weary curtain of sleet.

South and ever south they forced their way. They found a ford of the North Anna River in the afternoon and waded across. Snow fell, great soft white flakes. Hampton ordered another hour's halt as the gray light faded and darkness closed in.

The scouts ate the last hard cracker, the last morsel of Bob Dulin's smoked pork, the last crumb of cold corn bread brought by Hennegan and Schoolbred and Mikler. Shadburne questioned an old man and woman at a shantylike farmhouse, and returned.

"These folks say the Yankees got shoved back from Richmond by home guards," he told his friends. "They say Kilpatrick's in camp on the railroad—Atlee's Station, about two miles below us. Shoolbred, ride back and tell that to General Hampton."

On the rest of them rode, more slowly, quivering with anticipation. Hampton came to join them, accompanied by his young son and several couriers and staff officers. Clay, in advance of the group, wiped cold moisture from his eyes and rose in his stirrups to see more clearly in the dark.

"I see a fire down there," he reported.

"You're right," seconded Hampton, coming alongside. "It's their camp. Shadburne, hurry back and tell

Major Barker to slow up the main body. Carefully now, you other men, make as little noise as possible. Scott and Buckner, we three will go ahead and do some scouting ourselves."

Tensely they pushed on. Clay felt his skin tingle, his hair bristle. The fires there before them grew brighter and bigger.

"Stop," said Hugh Scott under his breath. "I saw a man on horseback yonder on the road."

Clay, too, made out the mounted figure, black against the foggy red glow of firelight beyond.

"It's their vidette on the road," pronounced Hampton. "Now then, you two wear blue. I want that vidette captured without the firing of a shot. Go on, both of you. I'll wait here to stop our men while you bring him in."

The two scouts rode on.

"How can we get him?" wondered Scott. "It's easy for a general to say grab him without a shot, but—"

"Let's take this little side road," suggested Clay. "Maybe we can get behind him, then come back toward him as if we were men from the camp."

"Good, Clay, you ought to be a general yourself."

They rode one behind the other on that narrow trail. The ground underfoot was deep with mud, and at one point they had to dismount and lead their horses. At last they emerged through a small clearing and back upon the road. Clay reconnoitered cautiously. Nobody could be seen toward the fires, and they knew that they were between the camp and the vidette.

"Now, act businesslike," said Hugh. "Let's come along side by side."

Mounting once more, they rode northward against battering sleet.

"Halt!" a cry hailed them. "Who goes there?"

"Relief," said Hugh Scott. "We'll take your place and give you a chance to get out of this storm."

"I'm glad to hear it."

They rode to the waiting figure.

"Why are there two of you?" asked the vidette.

"For safety's sake," replied Clay, coming close and suddenly thrusting his revolver under the man's nose. "You're our prisoner. Keep quiet and you won't get hurt."

Scott, on the vidette's other side, quickly snatched away his revolver, his saber, the carbine slung to his saddle. Then he seized the bridle reins.

"Keep your hands in the air," Clay cautioned the man. "Bring him along, Hugh."

They rode at a trot back to where Hampton waited with the other Iron Scouts and his staff.

"Lead that prisoner to the rear," directed Hampton. "No, not you, Scott. I still need you. Forward, you others. The point where that man was on guard will be the point for us to deploy against their camp."

≥ 3 ≤

"Happy Birthday"

Two colonels came to Hampton's side—Cheek of the First North Carolina, Andrews of the Second. Their bearded faces were dim through the falling snow as they listened to Hampton's confident, swift orders. Then they departed to dismount their commands, telling off every fourth man to hold horses. The troopers came forward on foot, long muskets ready in their hands. At the word of their officers they moved past the point where Hugh and Clay had taken the Federal vidette. Then they spread into a single line, weapons at the ready. Behind them two field guns rolled up. The gunners unslung these from their caissons, turned them around, and brought them forward by hand.

"Let the guns take the two ends of the line and keep trundling toward those fires," Clay heard Hampton say. "Now, advance—slowly—and keep formation. Not a word from anyone until I give the order. Then fire a volley into their camp and charge. And as you charge —yell your hearts out!"

Junior officers passed the word along. Clay rode close

to Hampton. "Shall we scouts dismount, too?" he asked.

"No," said Hampton at once. "Form up with my staff, like half a company of cavalry. We'll charge, too. Men on horses will add a different kind of scare."

"You figure on scaring them, General?" ventured Shadburne, and Hampton grinned quietly in his great beard.

"Scaring them is the only way," he replied. "Three hundred of us attacking more than three thousand of them—we need lots of surprise to even those odds."

The mounted men moved behind the cautiously advancing line. They could see the brightness of many fires ahead, with men huddling around them. Beyond were still more fires, and groups of tethered horses.

"We're about fifty yards off," said Hampton. "Shadburne, send two men to alert Colonel Andrews and Colonel Cheek. I'll fire my pistol as a signal to open the ball."

Shadburne waved Prioleau and Sloan away on the errand. Everyone waited silently, then saw the two messengers riding back. Hampton raised his revolver on high, and fired loud, bright flame into the night.

The revolver's crack was echoed by a concerted roar of muskets. An instant later came the boom of one cannon, then that of the other. After that rose the rebel yell, high, fierce, and quavering:

"Yieee-hee!"

"Let's get 'em, boys!"

The dismounted men ran forward on either side of the road.

"Charge!" thundered Hampton, and shook his bridle to start his own big horse dashing at the camp.

After him rode the Iron Scouts, the staff officers, and the couriers. As they galloped, they fired with revolvers. Clay's own weapon cracked, cracked again and yet again. Then they were into the camp.

All around them men sprang up from snow-shrouded blankets. One stumbled almost under the hoofs of Cherokee, who lifted himself and sprang over the crouching form. Bob Dulin's revolver spoke at Clay's ear, and Clay heard an exultant snarl from his friend who had vowed to reap one hundred lives in the war—he must have found his target.

Yells, floundering struggles, shattered the silence of the night on all sides.

"Surrender, Yank!" someone bellowed.

"Rally!" screamed a Northern voice. "Rally here, beat them off!"

Clay reached a huddle of horses under low-drooping branches. Two men were trying to untie a pair of mounts.

"Get away from those horses!" yelled Clay, firing his last shot. The two Federals turned and fairly shot away on foot, beyond the waving curtain of snow. Clay slid his empty revolver into its holster and fumbled for another in his saddlebag. On all sides the Union soldiers were running. One or two gray troopers paused by a fire, eagerly exploring a big kettle.

"They were boiling ham and potatoes here," cried one of them.

"And coffee in this other pot," added another.

"Get out of there, you hogs," snapped a sergeant, hastening by. "Win that food from the Yanks before you start swilling it down!"

Clay swung Cherokee between the tethered horses and another group of Federals. "Get going," he shouted at them. "These horses have been confiscated by the Confederate government!"

"Rally, men!" shouted a mounted officer beyond the mass of disorganized blue troopers, and Clay recognized the flat voice. He spurred forward and close, pointing his revolver.

"Surrender, General Kilpatrick," he called out.

"Not me, Johnny Reb!"

Kilpatrick snatched his own pistol from his belt. Clay pressed his trigger. Dully the hammer clicked. The charge was defective!

Next instant, fire seemed to bloom between him and the Federal general, and he felt as though a blacksmith had swung a hammer against his left arm between shoulder and elbow. He dropped his reins but tightened his knees to control Cherokee. Again he tried to fire, again his weapon failed. Kilpatrick raced away. Muskets crackled like popcorn on all sides.

"After him, boy," Clay bade Cherokee, but then he swayed weakly in his saddle. He dropped his revolver and caught the reins. He felt himself drooping forward toward Cherokee's mane.

"Clay!" came the anxious voice of Shadburne. "Are you all right?"

"All right," Clay tried to say, but his voice shook.

Shadburne's horse was close against Cherokee, Shadburne's arm was around Clay's waist.

"Hugh!" yelled Shadburne. "Hugh Scott! Help me get Clay down."

The battle rushed away somewhere, or perhaps Clay's ears grew dull to the noise. He shook his head dreamily. Hugh and Shadburne were half-lifting him from Cherokee's back.

"Sit down," Shadburne was saying. "Get your back to the tree there. That arm looks broken."

"General Kilpatrick shot me," Clay mumbled. "Kilpatrick himself."

He sat sagging against the tree. Shadburne found a blanket abandoned by one of the fleeing raiders, and wrapped it around Clay. Hugh darted to the nearest cooking fire and returned with a mug of hot coffee.

There was not so much gunfire now. The horse holders led their charges into the camp. Here and there roamed North Carolinians, plundering the tents and firesides.

Wade Hampton rode near. "We'll stop here," he called out. "No chance to follow them in this storm. Colonel Cheek, send out strong pickets, and tell those two gun crews to camp by their pieces." He reined in and looked down at Clay. "That's Buckner, isn't it? What happened to you, youngster?"

"Got hit in the arm, sir," said Clay, as Hugh offered him another sip of coffee.

"His arm's broken, General," supplemented Shadburne.

"Broken?" repeated Hampton. "Go find Dr. Wat Taylor and bring him here to take care of this boy. I couldn't have done without Buckner tonight." He leaned down. "Will you be all right?"

"Yes, sir," said Clay.

"Tell me, Buckner, how old are you?"

"Eighteen, sir. I'll be nineteen the tenth of this month."

"Nineteen on the tenth," Hampton repeated after him. "Happy birthday, Buckner!"

Dr. Taylor, the division's chief surgeon, came to examine Clay.

"Grit your teeth, young man," he said, and quickly and skillfully set the broken arm bone. He bound it tightly to two wooden splints and made a sling from a dark-blue silk scarf left behind by one of Kilpatrick's retreating officers.

"The bullet made a clean wound, and the fracture is a simple one," he pronounced. "We're just twelve miles from Richmond. You'll go there in a wagon with some other wounded. I'll send a report ahead, and they'll be ready for you at an army hospital."

"No army hospital for this man, sir," interposed Shadburne. "We have friends in Richmond who can look after him much better—a doctor's family, too. Clay, have them drop you off at the Winstead home."

"The Winstead home," repeated Clay somewhat dreamily, and Shadburne laughed.

"He knows a nice girl there," he said.

"A nice girl?" smiled Dr. Taylor. "Excellent. That ought to help him get well."

"And I'll see that your horse goes to the army stables in Richmond," offered Major Barker, joining the group. "He'll be well taken care of, and nobody will ride off on him while your bones are getting stuck back together."

"Here's a present for you and the Winsteads," added Hugh Scott. He shoved something round and heavy into Clay's inside pocket. "That's a bunch of Yankee greenbacks—better than a thousand dollars. I found it where one of Kilpatrick's officers bounced up and ran off without stopping to pick up his baggage."

As dawn broke, Hampton led the pursuit westward after Kilpatrick's big confused force, and Clay nursed his broken arm in an open wagon that carried half a dozen wounded to the Confederate capital.

Shadburne had given the driver careful directions. By noon the wagon trundled through streets in the northern part of town, and at length came to a halt before a two-story brick house with a flagstoned walk leading to the pillar-faced porch.

"This looks like the place," said the driver. "Let me help you down, son."

Carefully he did so. Clay still kept around his shoulders the blanket Shadburne had found for him in the captured camp. The driver walked with him to the front door and knocked.

A young girl opened to them. Her hair was black,

her eyes a bright blue, just as Clay had often remembered them.

"Is this Dr. Winstead's home?" the driver asked. "I understand you know this young fellow, and maybe you'll help him—"

"Lark," said Clay, wearily but happily.

"Clay Buckner!" Her hand came out to him. "You're wounded? Come in."

He followed her into the hallway. "Grandmother!" Lark Winstead called up the stairs. "Celie!"

Mrs. Winstead and Lark's beautiful young Aunt Celie hurried down like hoop-skirted whirlwinds. They smothered Clay with sympathy, bombarded him with questions. They almost carried him into a downstairs bedroom and seated him on a bed. Lark knelt to pull off his boots.

"You can't do that," Clay protested.

"Hold still," Lark half-scolded him. "There's one off—now the other."

"I'll have to cut this jacket off of you, Clay," said white-haired Mrs. Winstead. "It's only a blue Federal jacket anyway. Don't make faces like that, I've been a doctor's wife these forty years."

With a small sharp knife she slit the jacket's seams and dragged it free of his injured arm, his shoulder, then threw it aside. "Celie," she said, "bring one of the doctor's robes. And a basin of water, too; and soap and a towel. We'll have you in bed at once, Clay."

"Don't treat me as if I had a fever," he begged.

"We're going to see that you don't catch a fever," Mrs. Winstead assured him.

Within minutes he was loosely clad in the robe, lying propped on pillows with blankets over him. Mrs. Winstead had finished bathing his face, and combed back his tawny hair. Celie built a fire on the hearth. Lark had gone, but now she came back with a spoon and a steaming bowl.

"Soup," she informed him. "Open your mouth, Clay."

"Lark!" he fairly growled. "I'll be everlastingly dogged if you're going to feed me like a baby while I have one hand I can use. Give me that spoon."

She sat by the bedside, holding the bowl, while he gratefully dipped the savory broth. When he had finished, Clay smiled around at the three ladies.

"I feel ready to go back to duty now," he told them.

"That's the most foolish thing I've heard since Mr. Edgar Allan Poe's balloon hoax," snapped out old Mrs. Winstead. "You'll lie still and mend, young sir. Dr. Winstead is on duty at the army hospital, but he'll look at you when he comes home to supper."

"I feel fine," insisted Clay, but he yawned sleepily.

"You didn't put too much in the soup, did you, Lark?" asked Mrs. Winstead.

"You drugged me!" accused Clay, starting up from the pillows. Then he sagged back, yawning again.

"Just something to make you rest," said Mrs. Winstead, as though from far away, and soft, dark curtains seemed to close around Clay's eyes and ears and head.

When he awoke it was night. Old Dr. Winstead had

entered the room, with his wife and Lark carrying lamps. The white-haired doctor limped to the bedside, examined the dressing on Clay's arm, and probed with wise fingers.

"I don't see any inflammation around the wound, or flush on the cheeks," he decided. "Welcome to our home, young Mr. Buckner. It isn't the place you knew when we lived up in Northern Virginia, but it's comfortable —better far than the hospital."

"I don't know how to thank you all, sir," said Clay.

"We don't know how to thank you," the doctor assured him, "or any other brave man fighting for our country. Back to sleep now. Lark, do you know the address of Mr. Buckner's parents?"

"Northampton County, North Carolina," said Lark.

"Write them to say that their son was wounded in action, but that he is safe and in the hands of friends," her grandfather directed.

More sleep closed over Clay, and it was midmorning of the following day before he roused to surprise that he had slept so many hours.

He was able to rise and walk about the house. The furniture was handsome, burning fires made the rooms comfortable, but Clay knew that this household, like every other in the Confederate capital, was hard pressed for food and clothing. The Winstead table offered only such scanty meat, plain corn bread, and imitation coffee as Dr. Winstead, by virtue of his hospital service, was allowed to purchase from the commissary. Occasional onions and potatoes supplemented the fare. No other provisions could be secured save at staggering prices. The Winstead ladies refused the greenbacks Clay had brought until he swore that the money was a present from the Iron Scouts. Then Lark and Celie counted it on the round table in the drawing room.

"Eighteen hundred and ninety Federal dollars," Lark reckoned up. "That's a fortune. Worth twenty times that much in Confederate."

"It will be spent only for what we most badly need," proclaimed her grandmother, gathering up the bills. "Yes, and for help to our neighbors who aren't so fortunate."

But on Clay's birthday, the bright, chilly tenth of March, there was a delicious meat pie for noon dinner, and a fluffy brown cake.

"The frosting is made of molasses," apologized Lark.

"It's delicious," Clay told her, between mouthfuls.

The big front-door knocker rapped. Celie went to answer, and returned with shining eyes. Behind her walked a dark-bearded officer in gray, his hat in his gloved hand. Rising from the table, Clay felt a prodding sense of recognition.

"It's General Custis Lee," said Celie, and then Clay knew that he had seen the resemblance to Custis Lee's father, commander of the Army of Northern Virginia.

"I beg you, don't interrupt your meal," said the general. "No, ladies, I'll take nothing. Well, if you insist, a morsel of the cake only." He seated himself. "You say it is the birthday of this young man. I've come to see him on a matter of importance."

"Celie, Lark, come out of the room with me," commanded Mrs. Winstead, but Custis Lee raised his hand.

"No, all of you may listen. I know what service this household has done our army, and with what courage and discretion. I know I am able to speak openly before you."

"What do you want of me, General?" asked Clay.

Custis Lee studied him appraisingly. "You are the Iron Scout who brought the news of Kilpatrick's raid," he said. "General Hampton praised you as instrumental in foiling it."

"I was one of many, sir," said Clay. "I hope to go back to the army in a few days."

"And I hope you do not," Custis Lee told him. "I hope you will remain in Richmond to help us uncover a Federal spy."

"You think I could help?" cried Clay in amazement.

"It is still remembered how you worked here with General Winder last summer on a similar mission. Now, I command the defenses of Richmond, and the way those defenses must be maintained are countless. I need someone who is quick of eye and mind, who is not known to belong to the general staff or the provost guard, and who is completely loyal and dependable."

"Clay Buckner answers all of those requirements, General," said Lark Winstead boldly.

"Then," said Custis Lee, "if you will permit me, I shall ask your detachment to this temporary service." Again he looked searchingly at Clay. "With the temporary service goes a temporary commission as a lieutenant on my staff. Come to my headquarters tomorrow, and I will explain further what needs to be done, and how some of us think you can do it. Is it agreed?"

"At your orders, General," said Clay.

They rose and saluted each other.

❧ 4 ❧
High Society

Dressed in freshly polished boots, breeches, army shirt, and a cloak borrowed from Dr. Winstead, Clay appeared next morning at the Exchange Hotel where General Custis Lee maintained his headquarters. A brisk young aide took Clay's name, vanished awhile, then reappeared and escorted him into an inner room. Custis Lee glanced up from a paper-piled desk.

"Fetch Mr. Kingman," said Custis Lee to the aide, "and close that door as you go. Now, Buckner, sit here." Clay did so, and the general pushed a paper toward him. "That's your temporary commission as a second lieutenant for the duration of this assignment."

With one hand Clay folded the commission and stowed it in his shirt pocket. "I still don't understand the duty, sir."

"I've brought you here to explain." The handsome, dark-bearded face looked solemn. "Spies infest Richmond, and we're looking for one in particular, someone close to President Davis himself."

"Close to President Davis?" echoed Clay. "But how can that be possible?"

"We wonder the same thing. Somebody is informing the Federals of secret matters known only to the circle surrounding the President. We suspect that Kilpatrick's raid—the raid you helped turn back—was undertaken on just such special information."

"But the provost guard," said Clay. "Can't it trap this spy?"

"The provost guard is energetic, but its men are hardly suited to prowl through upper Richmond society. General Winder confessed as much, and then reminded us of how, last year, you caught that shrewd Yankee operative Tryon."

"I never caught Tryon," demurred Clay. "I only helped to chase him out of Richmond. He's somewhere with his friends now."

"Well, this spy must be caught," announced Custis Lee flatly. "You, Buckner, are presentable and mannerly. As an officer you'll be acceptable in any ballroom or at any tea or reception. You're sufficiently recovered, I hope, to receive the invitations I'll procure for you?"

"Dr. Winstead says that the splints can come off this arm in two weeks," Clay said. "In every other way I feel right healthy."

"I'll ask that you are made welcome in the home of Mrs. Marianne Parmenter," Custis Lee told him. "We suspect that it was in that very house that recent information was overheard and passed along by some guest who secretly spies for the Union."

"But—"

A knock at the door. "Come in," called Custis Lee, and a slender old man with long grizzled hair made his appearance. Over his arm were gray garments.

"Lieutenant Buckner, this is Mr. Kingman, a good tailor and a good friend," Custis Lee made the introductions. "I hope you'll be able to wear this uniform he brought you."

Clay rose from his chair. The tailor approached and held a pair of gray breeches against Clay's waist.

"A tolerable fit, considering I only guessed from your description," said Mr. Kingman to Custis Lee. "His boots look all right, General."

"They came out of the luggage of a Massachusetts captain," supplied Clay. "We captured it during the Mine Run campaign."

Mr. Kingman was holding out a tunic. Clay slid his uninjured arm into the sleeve, and the tailor pulled the tunic snugly over his other shoulder, letting it drape around the splinted arm. On the neat gray cuffs gleamed stripes of gold braid.

"It will do capitally," nodded Custis Lee. "Do you have a hat for Lieutenant Buckner, Mr. Kingman?"

The tailor departed to get it. Custis Lee rummaged in a corner closet and returned carrying a sword in a gold-mounted scabbard. Its hilt was gold, too, and dangled a gorgeous tassel.

"I'll lend you this," said the general, offering it. "My father presented it to me when I graduated at West Point."

"Sir, I'm doubly honored," said Clay gratefully, and took the beautiful dress sword in his hand. "I—I think—"

He stopped, not sure what he was trying to say. Mr. Kingman had come back. In one hand he carried two gray, plumed hats, and in the other a cape overcoat.

One of the hats fitted Clay well. Its brim was looped up smartly with a gleaming clasp that held a sweeping black plume. Setting it on his head before a mirror, Clay was reminded of the hat worn by General Jeb Stuart. Mr. Kingman put the overcoat upon Clay's shoulders. It was loose, but it would serve.

General Custis Lee smiled as Clay turned around.

"Lieutenant Buckner, you're a fine figure of an aide," he said, as Kingman left. "I vow that the proudest hostess in Richmond will be delighted to welcome you. Sit down again, and let's talk more of your assignment."

Talk he did, and very much to the point. Richmond, he reminded Clay, was a crowded, confused war capital, filled with strangers. These included officials, foreign observers, refugees from far places, speculators, blockade-runners, wounded soldiers, disguised deserters, and impostors. Numerous spies had been caught during the three years since the war had begun.

"But as I said earlier," finished the general, "the most dangerous of all those spies still operates, and in the vicinity of the President himself."

Again Clay tried to digest the information. "What sort of spy can he be?" he asked.

"We're not sure that it's a he. Women make capital spies, you know. We have our own ladies in the service, and they send us much valuable information."

"Yes, sir," agreed Clay. "We Iron Scouts are glad of their help."

"In any case," pursued Custis Lee, "this particular Federal agent keeps out of our sight and touch, so he— or she—must know about those of us who are searching. But you, Buckner, will be new in Richmond. Perhaps you can see without seeming to, hear without seeming to. Pretend to be just a young officer looking for pleasure instead of an Iron Scout looking for a spy."

He broke off, dipped pen in ink, and wrote swiftly. He blotted what he had written, folded it, and handed it to Clay.

"That," he said, "is a letter of introduction to Mrs. Parmenter. Now we must find a young lady for you to squire around."

"A young lady?" echoed Clay, staring.

"And a very pleasant young lady," elaborated Custis Lee. "Someone who can seem rather flutter-witted and gay, but who is at the same time intelligent and discreet. I wonder just who—"

He broke off, and knitted his brows in thought.

"General," Clay ventured after a moment, "perhaps I may suggest Miss Lark Winstead."

"Miss Lark Winstead?" repeated Custis Lee. "She's not been much in society, she has seemed more occupied with hospital work and charity among the families of poor soldiers. Hmmmm. . . . Yes."

"You think she would do, sir?"

"It would be very logical for you to be seen with her, the more since you are a guest at her home. It would be expected that the two of you might pay calls together. Is it your notion that she could be a help to us?"

"General, I heard you yourself praise the Winsteads for the way they helped the Confederacy when they lived behind the Union lines," Clay pointed out boldly. "I've been behind the Union lines, too. I've had occasion to see that Miss Lark is brave and coolheaded, as much so as any Iron Scout. And I'll go bail for her ability and loyalty."

"You are right," nodded Custis Lee. "I had not thought of anyone as young as Miss Lark Winstead; but her youth may make her less liable to suspicion. Very well, suppose you speak to her about this matter, but be certain that she keeps it to herself."

"Of course, General."

"Then, when you have met Mrs. Parmenter, when you are invited to the Parmenter home, Miss Winstead may be another pair of eyes and ears for us. Any questions, Buckner?"

"Only as to when I begin this spy hunting."

"You begin now, at once," Custis Lee informed him. "You've already begun."

Clay rose from his chair and saluted. Custis Lee smiled in his dark beard, very much a younger likeness of his father, and lifted his own hand to his brow.

"Suppose you go find Miss Winstead, and carry that introduction to the Parmenters," he said. "Leave your cloak, I'll have someone bring it out. Get used to your new uniform."

Clay departed. The borrowed sword, once a gift of Robert E. Lee to his son Custis, thudded its gold-clasped sheath against Clay's leg; the plume fluttered gracefully from his hat. On the street outside the hotel two young women looked admiringly at the trim figure Clay cut and whispered together. A plump young man in a black greatcoat and high silk hat accompanied them, and turned to sneer at Clay.

"Does your mother know you're out, sonny?" he called.

Clay stopped, swung around, and stared at the fellow.

"My mother knows right well that I'm out, sir," he snapped back. "She's known it ever since I left home a year ago to join the Army of Northern Virginia. I reckon the enlistment officers know equally well that you're not in. Look out, sir, they don't get you—times are so hard we're taking almost anything into the ranks these days."

The pudgy face went blank, then angry. "Why, you strutting little—"

"Hush, now, Cousin Emory," chided one of the young women. "He's been wounded in battle. I see the bandages there under his overcoat."

"Oh," said the plump one, contrite. "My apologies, Lieutenant."

Clay strode on. He must watch his temper, he told himself. A spy hunting for spies would do well to call no attention to himself.

Back at the Winstead house, he swung the big knocker at the door. Mrs. Winstead opened to him.

"Yes, sir?" she said, then looked at him in amazement. "Why, Clay! That uniform, that beautiful uniform—"

"It's just a loan, ma'am," Clay told her, stepping into the hall. Lark came running, to gaze wide-eyed in her turn.

"Let's sit down, the three of us," suggested Clay. "I have some right important and confidential news to share with you. You know part of it already, what General Custis Lee said yesterday. But there's more to tell and a favor to ask. Please swear to keep this a secret."

"We swear," said Mrs. Winstead. "Come into the parlor."

When the door was closed, Clay told Mrs. Winstead and Lark of his conversation with the general and the approval of his suggestion that Lark be asked to join him at spy hunting in Richmond's great houses.

"Me?" cried Lark uncomprehendingly.

"You should be proud to be asked, young miss," said her grandmother. "Aye, and happy, too, for opportunities to visit those gay gatherings."

"I have here a letter of introduction to Mrs. Marianne Parmenter," announced Clay, producing it. "It will include both of us, I think."

"Lark doesn't need any such introduction, Clay," Mrs. Winstead told him. "Indeed, Mrs. Parmenter and others have begged her to attend their receptions and musicales, but Lark has devoted her time to the hospitals and the relief committees."

"There's more reason for me to do such work than fritter my time away flirting and gossiping," said Lark, her chin lifting defiantly.

"I've wanted you to do something cheerful," reminded her grandmother, "and now it seems that there's a very good reason for you to accept invitations. After all, we Winsteads are just as good and old a name as Parmenter or—"

"All right, you don't have to persuade me," said Lark, and smiled at Clay, then at her grandmother. "The more you two talk, the more I feel as if I'd like a little fun."

"Fun!" snorted the old lady, and then she smiled— frostily, but still she smiled.

"Very good, child," she said, "there may be some fun along with the labor, and you'll enjoy it. I was such a one as you, forty years past, when young officers came a-calling."

"What young officers, Grandmother?" cried Lark eagerly.

"They're old officers now, those of them who are left," replied Mrs. Winstead, her face suddenly wistful with memory. "I remember Sam Cooper—"

"That white-haired adjutant general of the Confederacy?" asked Lark.

"But he was a lieutenant then," her grandmother said, "and his hair was dark, and he smiled and smiled. And there was Smith Lee, General Lee's older brother; a naval midshipman, he was then. Aye, and Lieutenant Albert Sidney Johnston—how handsome he was! They were as gallant as any we have today—"

She broke off. Her old eyes studied Clay. Then she smiled, with no frost in her smile this time, and slowly shook her head.

"I'm wrong, young people. Today is the day of the greatest gallantry. Let me say a word. This conversation is at an end, and we'll not talk any more of what you two are up to, unless there's a real need. Lark, come with me. We must get you finery to match that new gold braid on Clay's coat."

The finery was not too hard to produce. Many homes in Richmond had only threadbare dresses for the ladies who lived in them, but the Winsteads had remained in the very environs of Washington until the summer of 1863, and both Lark and her pretty Aunt Celie had frocks that never had been worn in Richmond.

Mrs. Winstead found a dark-green dress with a hoop skirt like a great flounce-trimmed bell. A jacket of the same cloth, with cuffs turned back, set the dress off. Celie contributed a hat of beaver and a foxskin muff. Everyone admired Lark when she and Clay stood waiting for the hired hack that would take them to Mrs. Parmenter's.

"You'll smash the heart of every young spark in Richmond, Lark," vowed Celie. "I still don't understand why you've suddenly left your hospital work for society."

"Clay talked me into it," replied Lark, and Clay meditated that she told the exact truth, though not all of it—good policy for the spy service. "He has a letter for Mrs. Parmenter," Lark went on, "and he doesn't know the Parmenters and I do, so—"

She made an explanatory gesture. Celie nodded brightly. Apparently she had forgotten all about the visit of Custis Lee the day before.

"Then enjoy yourselves," she bade the two. "Here's your carriage at the door. Gracious, Mother, how handsome Clay is as a lieutenant! I'm tempted to claim seniority over Lark, and drive out with Clay in her place."

As they opened the door, Lark paused to look back at her aunt.

"What if a fine, noble sergeant were to call?" she asked.

"I'd take him," confessed Celie, eyes sparkling, "particularly if he were Sergeant Shadburne of the Iron Scouts!"

Clay handed Lark into the hack and got in beside her. Lark gave the driver directions, and away they rolled.

The Parmenter home was on Grace Street, a massive and lofty house of cut gray stone behind brick walls that reminded Clay of a fortress. He paid the hack driver with three Confederate dollars, then escorted Lark through a wrought-iron gate and up on a porch with big fluted pillars. At their knock the door was opened by a dark butler in a frock coat, dignified enough to be one of President Davis' cabinet officers.

"What name shall I say?" he intoned ceremoniously.

"I have here a letter for Mrs. Parmenter."

Clay offered the envelope. The butler took it in his big brown hand and studied it as though it might explode.

"Please come into the drawing room," he invited, more grandly than before, and opened the door wide.

Clay and Lark found themselves in a high-ceilinged chamber that seemed full of exquisitely fragile furniture.

"I'm afraid to sit down," whispered Lark. "The legs of those chairs look like matchsticks."

"Expensive matchsticks," agreed Clay.

A great hospitable peal of contralto laughter smote their ears, and into the drawing room swept an overwhelming personage, all high-piled blond hair and plump pink shoulders and tossing skirts. A pudgy hand, blazing with jewels, caught at Lark's wrist.

"You've come to call on me at last!" cried the contralto voice. "Well, young Miss Winstead, it couldn't be higher time. And this gentleman—?"

Proud, bright eyes turned on Clay, like the muzzles of two challenging guns.

"This is Lieutenant Buckner," Lark said.

"I came with a note for Mrs. Parmenter, ma'am," Clay managed.

"Note?" She waved it in her other hand. "Oh, yes, yes indeed! I have it here—from dear General Lee, General Custis Lee, I mean." She examined the note again, so closely and intently that Clay wondered if Mrs. Marianne Parmenter were not nearsighted, and too vain to wear spectacles. "And you—yes, you're Lieutenant Buckner, it says."

She looked at him again, and her eyes were cordial now.

"You are from North Carolina, I believe?"

"I live in Northampton County, ma'am."

"Ah yes, Northampton County." She let go of Lark's wrist and tamped a finger against her round chin. "That's practically Virginia. You must know the Burgwyns and the Ransoms, and the Longs of Longview—"

"I'm somewhat kin to the Longs, ma'am," Clay told her. "And you, I presume, are Mrs. Parmenter?"

"Oh!"

Her laughter rang out, as loud and vibrant as bells ringing an alarm. "Oh!" she cried again. "You must forgive me, Lieutenant Buckner, but Lark and I know each other, and I forgot that you were a stranger. Yes, yes, I am Mrs. Marianne Parmenter."

Her plump, dimpled hand caught his and pumped it vigorously.

"And here," she said, as someone else came in, "this is my niece, Rowena. Rowena dear, allow me to present Miss Lark Winstead and Lieutenant—uh—yes, of course, Lieutenant Clay Buckner." She beamed at Clay. "Miss Rowena Croft, Lieutenant."

Rowena Croft was as blonde as her aunt, and almost as formidably cordial; but where Mrs. Parmenter was plumply short, Rowena Croft stood almost as tall as Clay. She smiled, showing the whitest of teeth between the reddest of lips, as Clay bowed to her. Dark brows slanted above her blue eyes.

"And Lieutenant Buckner is a kinsman of the Longs of Longview," prattled Mrs. Parmenter helpfully.

"Indeed?" said Rowena Croft, in a deep cooing voice. Her eyes studied Clay carefully, even appraisingly; never, he thought, had an inspecting officer so examined him from head to foot. He felt, rather than saw, Lark draw herself up stiffly at his elbow. The blue eyes of Rowena Croft fixed on his arm in its sling.

"And you are wounded," she added, as though he did not know it.

"I'm mending well, thank you, ma'am," said Clay.

"He's on Custis Lee's staff, Rowena," burbled Mrs. Parmenter. "Stationed here in Richmond. That means he's available."

"Available?" asked Lark, almost sharply, and their hostess went off into another clanging peal of laughter.

"Oh, what did I say?" she demanded of the ceiling.

"My aunt and I are at a loss for young gentlemen for our theatricals," explained Rowena Croft.

"Yes, that's what I meant by available," elaborated Mrs. Parmenter. "Lieutenant Buckner is so handsome, he must appear. Aye, sir, you must, I'll not hear a refusal."

"But I'm no play actor, ma'am," Clay protested.

"Tut, sir, none who watch will know the difference."

"It will be only a series of tableaux," said Rowena Croft. "Perhaps I should say charades."

"And it is for the benefit of our wounded soldiers,"

chimed in Mrs. Parmenter. "Dear Rowena, where is that girl, Psyche? She must fetch us tea—the real tea from the blockade-runner, none of your mint leaves this afternoon. Please sit down, Lieutenant. And you, Lark, my dear."

She swept out of the room. "Psyche!" they heard her call. "Tea, Psyche!"

"Sit here," invited Rowena Croft, gesturing Clay to a sofa. As he sat down, she moved gracefully to his side and took her place there. Lark found a chair opposite, and put her hands in her lap. One of them was doubled into a small fist.

Clay told himself that this was nothing like prowling unfamiliar ground at the edge of the Yankee army with Shadburne and the Iron Scouts; but it was unfamiliar ground, at that. And Lark, at least, seemed to feel that it was hostile ground.

≽ 5 ≼

Rumors and Compliments

Tea came, delicate china cups on a silver tray almost as big as an artillery wheel and borne by a dark, turbaned maid as lofty-mannered as the butler in the hall. Mrs. Parmenter fluttered like a blonde partridge, coaxing Clay and Lark to take sugar lumps and sliced lemon.

"We'll stun the town and dazzle society," she announced between bites of cake hearty enough for a hungry soldier. "The town chatters about Mrs. Ives and her play to raise funds—that was *The Rivals* by Sheridan. Oh, not that awful Yankee, Phil Sheridan, but Richard Brinsley Sheridan, you know." She laughed, and Clay wondered if she had made a joke. "And she had Mrs. Clement Clay and Captain John Randolph, and Constance Cary was lovely as Lydia." She blinked fondly at her niece. "No more lovely than you would have been in the part, Rowena dear."

"And you, Aunt Marianne, would have outshone Mrs. Clay," drawled Rowena.

"I?" challenged Mrs. Parmenter. "I play Mrs. Malaprop, that foolish old woman, with all Richmond looking on? Never!"

"That play is past, and our evening of charades is in the future," said Rowena. Her blue eyes fixed on Clay. "You have done charades, Lieutenant Buckner?"

"Why, not lately, ma'am. Only as a boy at school."

"Really?" prompted Lark. "You never told me that, Clay."

"I remember once," said Clay, "we got hold of a little yellow cur dog. One of us handed him to another boy, who had feathers in his hair to look like an Indian chief. Then the other side—we'd divided into two parties—had to guess what it meant."

"And what did it mean?" inquired Rowena, her voice softer and deeper than ever.

"Handkerchief," spoke up Lark, almost fiercely.

"Eh?" demanded Mrs. Parmenter. "What was that?"

"Hand the cur to the chief," explained Lark, like a patient teacher with a dull pupil. "Handkerchief."

"I vow!" Another peal of Mrs. Parmenter's laughter. "That was witty."

"But you all want something more elaborate than that," ventured Clay, sipping the hot, fragrant tea.

"Of course," agreed Rowena. "Something to please a real society audience, something with real theatrical scenery and costuming. I've been thinking as we talk here—"

"So have I," put in Lark.

"Have you so?" inquired Mrs. Parmenter brightly.

"Rowena, do help Lieutenant Buckner to more cake. Now, Lark dear, what is your inspiration?"

"The word is pilgrimage," said Lark. "For the first syllable, dramatize a doctor with a pill. For the second, something grim—maybe poor beggars being spurned by a rich miser. For the third, a scene of old age. Then the whole word for a final scene, pilgrims and music and a tableau."

"Capital!" applauded Mrs. Parmenter, her pudgy palms striking together. "Rowena, will you bring forward an idea as good?"

"My word is industrial," announced Rowena. "For the whole word we can show a party of ladies rolling bandages and cutting uniforms. For the first syllable —in—we can have an inn, with guests arriving, gay blades flirting with the hostess, and so on. The second syllable is dust, and we can stage a burial scene—"

"No, no, too many in the audience will have lately seen the burial of kinsmen and friends," demurred her aunt.

"Then have servants sweeping and dusting," suggested Clay.

"You are truly helpful, Lieutenant Buckner." Rowena fairly purred, and from the corner of his eye Clay saw Lark clench her fist again. "The third scene will be trial, and that should be dramatic enough, with a prisoner and a court and a judge."

"Judge Robert Ould shall preside in that scene," decided Mrs. Parmenter. "He dare not refuse us. Who else can we count on? The Cary girls must come, they were in Mrs. Ives' play. Then we'll ask Agnes De Leon to lend us her Oriental scarfs and jewels and cloaks. And Mrs. Semmes and Mrs. Chesnut and others will help."

"We will have plenty of ladies," nodded Rowena. "I am more interested in gentlemen."

"I daresay," muttered Lark, and Clay flinched in embarrassment for her, but the others did not hear.

"Each of you must plan and stage your charade," said Mrs. Parmenter. "Let the audience try to guess the word, and vote on which is most original."

She hopped up from her chair and pulled open a pair of great double doors. A room larger than the parlor could be seen beyond, richly furnished and hung with beautiful drapes. At its far end stood a low platform, such as might be used by musicians at a ball or private concert.

"We'll hang velvet curtains to draw wide or pull shut," cried Mrs. Parmenter, gesturing. "Tallow candles will make footlights. The chairs will be set in rows, all the way back here into the parlor. After our charades we'll remove the chairs for a dance, and the supper table will be set across the hall there." Again she clapped her hands. "I must write down those two charades as you girls told them to me. And I'll lock the paper in my desk, and none of you must whisper them anywhere. Let them remain secret until the night!"

Rowena was looking at Clay again. "Lieutenant," she said, "you have not told us how you came by your wound."

"That was when Kilpatrick came riding down," said Clay.

"Yes," contributed Lark. "All of the Richmond defense troops, even staff officers, had to hurry out when the raiders came close."

In his heart Clay thanked Lark for her quick explanation. Not yet was he perfect in the role of a noncombatant on duty at the capital. He rose to leave before another question trapped him.

"I fear we must go," he said to Mrs. Parmenter. "I have an errand to run for General Custis Lee."

"But you will return, young sir," Mrs. Parmenter gushed. "My niece and I hope to see much more of you."

"Perhaps Lieutenant Buckner would come to dinner some night soon, and help us further with our plans for the charades," put in Rowena. "Where do you lodge, Lieutenant?"

"Clay is a guest at our home," Lark replied, and Rowena turned to survey Lark narrowly, as though she were a dangerous enemy. Hastily Clay bowed himself out of the parlor and the house. He and Lark walked toward the center of town.

"And I hope that you have a very good dinner indeed, Lieutenant Buckner," Lark drawled in mocking imitation of Rowena's voice. "Just because Rowena Croft was named for Ivanhoe's queen of love and beauty, she seems to feel sure—"

But Clay had turned around as the cry of a newsboy caught his ear. He quickly beckoned the shabby lad to him and bought a paper. He scowled as he looked at the first page.

"Ulysses S. Grant," he read, half-aloud. "He's going to command the Army of the Potomac against us."

"Another Yankee commander," said Lark.

"More than just another Yankee commander. Grant captured Fort Donelson out west. He won the Battle of Shiloh from us when we'd practically won it from him, and he forced Vicksburg to surrender. Not only that, but he'll have something more than a hundred thousand troops under him—"

Then he looked up. "I'm sorry, Lark, I was woolgathering and not listening to you. What did you say?"

"Nothing of any importance whatever," Lark assured him. "Look yonder, there comes a hack. Signal for it to take us home."

Next morning, when Clay reported at the office of General Custis Lee, he found a note from Mrs. Parmenter awaiting him.

The company of Lieutenant Clay Buckner was requested at dinner the following Thursday evening. A number of Mrs. Parmenter's friends would be present, and Mrs. Parmenter begged to hope that Lieutenant Buckner would take pleasure in making their acquaintance. Lark was not included in the invitation, and when Clay showed it to her at the Winstead home that evening she sniffed almost as fiercely as her grandmother.

"That's Mrs. Parmenter's signature, I suppose," she said, "but it's Rowena Croft's invitation. I saw her studying your scalp and thinking how nice it would look at her belt."

"She's no hostile Indian," laughed Clay in protest.

"No Indian, perhaps, but she's hostile. I'd not be surprised if it turned out that she was that Yankee spy we're after."

"Hush, not so loud," begged Clay. "If she's a spy, you can arrest her."

Dinner at Mrs. Parmenter's was pleasant, at that. The party included a South Carolina newspaper editor and his soft-voiced young wife, a mannerly official of the Tredegar Iron Works in charge of experimenting with new cannon, a most resolute-seeming lady who worked hard in the Richmond military hospitals, and a lean, short-bearded man of perhaps forty in civilian clothes. This man walked with a cane, as though one leg was injured or weakened, and his eyes were black and shadowed.

"Major Towers," Mrs. Parmenter introduced him. "He's from 'way off in Texas or Arkansas or somewhere like that."

"From Missouri," amended Major Towers, smiling at Clay, "and lucky to be here. I'm a long way from home, and the whole Yankee nation stands between me and there."

At the table—the main course was a delicious roast turkey, which Mrs. Parmenter proudly informed her guests had cost thirty-four Confederate dollars—the major told of the adventures which had brought him to Richmond.

"Grant took Vicksburg, and that left my part of the Confederacy cut off from the rest of the country," he explained. "It also left a big herd of cattle—three thousand—that was supposed to be delivered to the troops in Mississippi. We knew that those boys were hungry for beef, and that we were honor bound to get it to them. Finally I drew the assignment to drive the herd across the Mississippi some way, but nobody told me how I was to do it."

"And what was your device, Major Towers?" inquired Rowena, who sat beside Clay and was cutting up the turkey on his plate.

"I taught three steers to swim," he replied, smiling in his beard. "Got them used to jumping into the water of a bayou and paddling right across to the far side. Then I hired six men with horses to help me, and we drove the herd down to the river with those three swimmers leading the way. In they jumped like bullfrogs, and the rest after them. Across we went to the east bank. Didn't lose a hoof or horn."

Applause went all around the table.

"And so your troubles were all over," bubbled Mrs. Parmenter.

"No, ma'am, I found they'd just begun. We ran into a patrol of Forrest's cavalry and told them we were bound for army headquarters at Jackson, Mississippi. They almost shot us down for Yankees."

"Because the Yankees were in Jackson," suggested Clay.

"Exactly. The Confederates had evacuated and gone

east. Finally I persuaded the boys that we were on their
side, and they agreed to get the cattle to the new headquarters. So I paid off my helpers and followed the
herd along to make delivery. I got shot by a Federal
scout on the way, right through the knees. Spent months
in a hospital in Montgomery, then went to Atlanta, and
finally came up here where the real war seems to be
going on."

"I thought it was going on nearly everywhere," observed Rowena.

"But I'm not back in it yet," complained Towers.
"I'm almost ready to walk again, or at least ride, but I
haven't found an assignment."

"You underwent a real Odyssey," remarked the South
Carolina editor.

"It was more like an Anabasis," offered Clay, "with
three thousand cattle instead of ten thousand Greeks."

Faces looked at Clay above the dishes and the candle-
sticks. Mrs. Parmenter seemed mystified, Rowena to
admire, Towers friendly.

"Egad, here's a learned young officer," said the artil·
lery expert. "Lieutenant Buckner—that's your name,
eh? Have you a tale of daring to tell us?"

"A staff officer has no chance to be daring," Clay assured the company.

"Lieutenant Buckner was wounded fighting the Kilpatrick raiders," Rowena spoke up, as though defending him, "and he's too modest to tell about it."

"It could have happened to anyone unlucky enough
to be where I was," Clay said. "A Yankee soldier

jammed his gun almost against me and fired. It might have been my head instead of my arm. I can do my staff work one-handed."

"And you are to be a one-handed actor in my charades," Mrs. Parmenter reminded him again.

After dinner another group of guests arrived. Most of these were ladies, and Clay bowed and murmured politely as he was introduced to the stately wife of Senator Thomas Semmes of Louisiana and to the dazzling Constance Cary, who arrived under escort of President Davis' secretary, Burton Harrison. Also there, like crinolined nymphs, were girls whose names he heard as Evelyn Cabbell, Mary Triplett, Hetty Cary, and Sally Enders. Mrs. Parmenter gathered them in her parlor like a group of conspirators, then produced from her desk the notes on the charades Lark and Rowena had suggested.

"I will call on every one of you to help," she warned. "Remember, this is to raise money for the relief of soldiers' families. Our audience will include President Davis himself and his lady. On our stage will appear the loveliest girls in Richmond and some of the bravest men."

Rowena's blue eyes twinkled at Clay.

"I expect Lieutenant Buckner to assist with my charade," she announced. "My symbolic pantomime of the word industrial."

"But—" began Clay.

"Oh," she said, smiling no more, "did Miss Lark Winstead speak first, to enlist you in her charade?"

"No, as a matter of fact she didn't say anything about that, but—"

Clay was not sure what he was protesting, and he was spared the embarrassment of pausing to invent an excuse, for Mrs. Parmenter began to talk again.

"I must insist that you help Rowena," she told Clay. "We cannot lag back in this cause." She might have been speaking of the defense of Richmond itself. "He will be in your company, Rowena."

"How many charades in all?" inquired one of the ladies.

"Three, I think," replied Mrs. Parmenter. "The two by Lark Winstead and my niece, and one which I myself shall offer. It need not have so many actors, indeed only two in all. Myself and a gentleman." She smiled at Major Towers. "I conscript you, Major."

He bowed and smiled back at her. "Enchanted, ma'am."

"And we must tell nobody, not even these others, what it is. Please come sit beside me, sir. I'll whisper in your ear."

He moved his chair close to her. Her hand cupped to his ear while she muttered. He nodded, as though in admiration and approval.

"Splendid," he praised.

The party came to an end. As Clay paid his compliments and said his farewells, Major Towers joined him.

"Which way are you bound, Lieutenant Buckner?"

"To the center of town," said Clay. "I must report each morning and evening to General Custis Lee at the

Exchange. Then I'll go to the Winstead home, where I lodge."

"I'll walk with you as far as the Exchange," offered Towers.

They strolled together along the street. Major Towers managed a brisk pace, his cane tapping the pavement. Clay saw that it was a handsome one of dark polished wood, ringed with a band of silver below the crooked handle.

"Young man," said the major, "you don't have the air of a smug, self-complacent little staff officer."

"That's my assignment, sir," replied Clay. "I try to meet it to the best of my ability, and I hope it amounts to some sort of service to the Confederacy."

"Don't be politely resentful," protested Major Tower lightly. "I meant to compliment you. I feel that you have a little of the same chafing spirit that's in me. You're here in Richmond, but you'd much prefer to be in the field."

There was truth in those words, and Clay reflected that his companion had a shrewd eye and a shrewder mind.

"You've guessed the right of it, Major," he decided to confess. "However, I'm where I am at the express wish of General Custis Lee himself."

"Then you're someone he likes and trusts and values."

"That's not for me to say, sir," replied Clay.

"The chill is back in your voice, Lieutenant, and that's not seemly from a junior officer to a senior. Well, I'll be frank: I'm without a command since I was cut off from my comrades in the Trans-Mississippi District. Might I ask a favor?"

"Ask it, sir," said Clay.

"You're wondering if you can grant it." Major Towers chuckled again. "This is all I seek. Please ask General Custis Lee if he will give me an interview, and perhaps help me to an appointment where I can be of use, too."

Clay nodded. "I'll give him that message."

"You put me in your debt. And yonder is the Exchange Hotel. Wait until I write my address—I'm at the Spotswood. Good night, Lieutenant Buckner, and we'll see each other as we rehearse those charades of Mrs. Parmenter's."

≽ 6 ≼
Rehearsal

General Custis Lee readily agreed to interview Major Towers, and after the major had gone Lee called Clay in to talk about the stranger from Missouri.

"An able and intelligent officer if I ever met one," said the general at once. "I judge that things beyond the Mississippi are slightly informal, but your Major Towers would do credit to any army. That story of bringing the cattle across the river—" Custis Lee's smile was an admiring endorsement.

"Sir," ventured Clay, "how were his papers of identification?"

"They're all in perfect order," Custis Lee told him. "Signed by General Kirby Smith. Towers has asked for staff duty at army headquarters in the field, and I'm inclined to recommend him. What do you think, Buckner?"

"Since you ask me, General, I do have a suggestion. Don't send along that recommendation until after Mrs. Parmenter's charades have been presented."

The smile left the general's face, to be succeeded by a

frown of mystified surprise. "She seems to have convinced you, along with half of Richmond's society sparks, that those charades are more important than the conduct of the war. We have reports that Grant's gathering a huge army up in the Wilderness to strike us, and we need every officer and man—Major Towers and you, maybe myself, if they'd transfer me from this office."

"I just got a note from Mrs. Parmenter that the charades will be shown next Thursday night," pleaded Clay. "Major Towers is an important part of her show, and maybe these last few days will allow his wounded leg to heal more fully. And there are other considerations, too."

Custis Lee studied his young aide. "Other considerations?" he repeated. "I daresay there are. All right, Towers stays in Richmond until the charades are over. He paid you a compliment, by the way—said you seem too good for gilded staff work. Tell him I'm looking for a place for him, and that I'll be at Mrs. Parmenter's to see if these charades are as significant as everybody insists."

Clay's discussion with Lark Winstead was not so calm. When he said that he had been assigned to Rowena Croft's charade, Lark's eyes blazed like signal lights starting a night bombardment.

"I'll wager you didn't protest," she scolded him.

"I only started to," admitted Clay. "She and her aunt talked me down. Anyway, things are better with me in that part of the show."

"Better for which of us?" demanded Lark. "You, me, or Rowena?"

"For everyone, Lark. That party will see everybody in President Davis' immediate circle in attendance. The Davises, cabinet officers, undersecretaries, generals. A prime group for this unknown spy to watch and question, maybe to probe for new secrets."

"But if you're with Rowena, and I—"

"There'll be two big casts for the two charades," pointed out Clay. "You'll work closely with one, I with the other. We can discover any suspects more easily."

She nodded in unsympathetic agreement. "But remember," she said, "if Rowena Croft is the spy, I'm to arrest her. You promised."

"If she's the spy, I'll want to watch you arrest her," laughed Clay, but Lark did not join in.

At the Parmenter house on Saturday for the first rehearsals, Clay passed on to Major Towers the message of Custis Lee.

"I said you'd place me in your debt, and you have," said Towers. "Look here, if I go to army headquarters —to the staff of Robert E. Lee—how would you like to come along? Once I was there, I could quickly arrange it."

The staff of Robert E. Lee. . . . Clay knew a moment of dazzled and fanciful visions of what that might mean. But next moment he remembered the Iron Scouts, a service equally useful and one for which he had proved his fitness again and again.

"I reckon I'm needed right where I am," he said.

"And where are you, Lieutenant?"

"He's in the first syllable of my charade," replied Rowena for Clay, as she came toward them. "Come with me, Lieutenant. Meet some of the others who'll help us portray the inn."

The double doors had been closed, and while Rowena rehearsed her companions in the parlor, Lark gathered hers out of sight in the ballroom. All eyes in the parlor turned upon Rowena, who looked very conscious of how pretty she was.

"Others will come Thursday night to be guests at the inn," she said, "and we will be the servants and proprietors. Where's Captain Page McCarthy?"

"At your service, ma'am," spoke up a young officer.

"You'll have to put an apron over that fine uniform and act as the bartender," Rowena informed him. "Now for a bootboy."

"May I do that?" asked Clay. "I can slide a boot over this bandaged arm and polish it with the other hand."

"Capital," approved Rowena. "An apron for you, too, and a dirty one. Choose it from those things on the chair. The landlord—oh dear, we're short on men. Judge Ould says he will appear in only one syllable."

"Suppose you be the hostess," suggested a handsome lady.

"No, Mrs. Webb, I say you'll take that part," said Rowena. "I'll be barmaid."

"Now there's a barmaid who could have me for a customer all day long," muttered Captain McCarthy to Clay.

They rehearsed, and rehearsed again to grow confident in the parts. Standing behind a buffet representing a bar, Captain McCarthy made energetic play with imaginary bottles and mugs. Rowena bustled here and there, and Mrs. Webb presided with stern grandeur. Clay knelt in a corner, going through the motions of polishing.

"How will the audience know it's an inn?" asked a graceful old gentleman with white hair.

"They mustn't find it too easy to guess, Colonel Deas," replied Rowena. "We'll have a sign, of course; Major Willie Caskie has promised to paint me one. Very well, that's enough for the present. We'll do our innkeeping until I clap my hands." She struck them smartly together by way of illustration. "Then the curtains will draw, and we'll make ready for the next syllable. That's dust, and I'll want your help, Colonel Deas. You'll try to get away from me as I dust. Shall we rehearse?"

The others laughed at the pantomime. The third syllable, trial, called for a simulated courtroom. This time the buffet did duty as the judge's desk, and behind it presided Judge Robert Ould, the dignified commissioner for exchange of prisoners. Clay was told off to be the prisoner, with Captain McCarthy as sheriff, Burton Harrison as prosecutor, and Colonel Deas as attorney for the defense. The supposed men of law made dumb show of arguments, the judge rapped sternly for order.

"And the whole word is industrial," said Mrs. Webb at the end of the scene.

"That needs no rehearsing," said Rowena. "I've invited a sewing circle to come and work for our audience to watch. There'll be the Cary girls, the Triplett girls, the Enders sisters, and half a dozen others. Who knows? We may finish a whole uniform for some brave soldier while we're putting on a show for relief of that soldier's family."

The other group had finished its practice, and Mrs. Parmenter appeared to open the double doors once more and to summon her servants with trays of cake made with dried peaches, while she herself poured cups of coffee brewed from ground okra seed.

"Major Towers and I rehearsed in my music room," she gurgled with coy laughter. "We defy the world to guess our charade."

"Animal, vegetable, or mineral?" inquired Judge Ould.

"All three," answered Major Towers, his silver-ringed walking stick lying across his knees as he balanced his cup and saucer.

Lark remembered that cryptic exchange as she and Clay made their way home. "Animal, vegetable, or mineral," she repeated. "Rowena Croft is none of the three; she's just a blinking, simpering doll. I'm going to make Aunt Celie come into my charade and help me out."

When they entered the Winstead home, Lark asked for Celie.

"She's out in the kitchen," Mrs. Winstead informed them. "Someone's with her, waiting to say hello to both of you."

They hurried to the kitchen together. Sergeant George Shadburne's brown beard wagged at them above a plate of biscuits and honey which Celie had just handed him. He smiled at the happy greeting of Lark, and shook Clay's uninjured hand.

"I just thought I'd sit out here, away from any chance callers, and give Clay the latest news from the front," he said. "I arrived after dark with a report from cavalry headquarters. When can we expect you back, Clay? There's plenty of work on hand for everyone."

"I expect to be out of these splints in a week at most," replied Clay, "and out of a little special chore the Richmond headquarters gave me about the same time."

"Stay until Thursday, Sergeant George," begged Lark, "and be in my charade. I want to outdo a certain Richmond belle who's ringing mighty loud and brassy in my ears."

"I can't stay," Shadburne told her. "I'll be riding back before the hour's out. Clay, the boys have shivered and scrambled all over the ground between the armies, and plenty of times back of the Union lines. I don't know when Grant expects to move, but when he does there'll be trouble enough to give two helpings to every soldier in the Confederacy."

He explained the positions of the opposing armies. They were somewhat as they had been a year ago—in Northern Virginia, between Richmond and Washington—but this time they faced each other across the Rapidan River instead of the Rappahannock. Culpeper Court House, once a Confederate stronghold and familiar to the Iron Scouts, was headquarters for the new Federal commander. From here and there Shadburne, Hogan, Scott, Shake Harris, and the others had gleaned information to indicate that the new invading force would number nearly a hundred and twenty thousand, with thirty thousand more under General Benjamin F. Butler on the Virginia Peninsula to eastward.

"That means a hundred and fifty thousand, more than Joe Hooker fetched against us at Chancellorsville last May," summed up Shadburne. "They have twelve thousand cavalry, and enough wagon trains of ammunition and provisions to reach sixty-five miles along a road."

"And General Lee?" prompted Celie. "What force can he bring?"

"Perhaps sixty or seventy thousand," Shadburne told her soberly. "A few more regiments may come up from the Carolinas, but they'll all be needed to fend Butler off while we others stand in Grant's way. Our cavalry will come to something around six thousand if General Hampton is lucky enough to get the South Carolina recruits he wants. This new campaign means odds of two to one against us."

"The odds were two to one against us at Chancellorsville," Clay remembered, "and we chased Fighting Joe Hooker clear out of Virginia."

"That's right, we did," nodded Shadburne, stroking his beard. "You and I were there and helped some, didn't we? But from what I reckon about this new fellow Grant, he's a different man from Hooker. He does about a quarter as much talking, and makes up the difference by fighting."

"That was in the west," argued Celie stoutly. "He never had to fight Lee and the Army of Northern Virginia."

"And we still have the same leaders that defeated Hooker," added Lark. "Longstreet, Jeb Stuart, A.P. Hill—"

"But we don't have Stonewall Jackson," put in Clay. "He's been missed every single day since he died. I'd feel safer if old Stonewall was up there, right where Grant least expected to find him."

"And I'd feel safer if you were up there, too," Shadburne said honestly. "When do you figure you can jump on that horse of yours and ride back to the Iron Scouts?"

"Give him another week, Sergeant," Dr. Winstead answered for Clay as he, too, entered the kitchen. "His arm is healing nicely, and the splints can come off soon. He may not have full use of his arm at once, but he can ride and scout."

"I have to be here until Thursday, at least," said Clay.

"Oh, yes," teased Lark. "Let him stay until Thursday, by all means. Clay's become the greatest actor in Richmond, Sergeant George, most sought after in high society. He's in one of those charades I told you about, surrounded by pretty girls. One in particular."

Shadburne glanced at Lark, then at Celie. "She's not as pretty as you two, I'll be bound," he ventured.

"This girl is too pretty to be true," Lark fairly snapped out, "and so she's not what I'd call true."

Shadburne laughed heartily, and so did Dr. Winstead. Celie brought out more biscuits and honey for all.

"Our camp's above the Rappahannock, at Captain Crofut's farm," Shadburne told Clay. "We're in the woods back of the captain's house."

"I know Crofut's place well," Clay said eagerly, "above Barrett's Ford."

"Don't cross at Barrett's Ford," warned Shadburne quickly. "There's a lot of Federal picket prowling thereabouts. Swim your horse over the Rapidan above there, and come up after dark if you can. But you'd better sing when you ride in. You don't want the boys to take you for one of Sheridan's scouts."

"Not for a moment I don't," agreed Clay. "Not with Bob Dulin so anxious to run his score up higher, and me looking Yankeefied in the nighttime. What shall I sing?"

"Name a song for him, ladies," requested Shadburne.

Celie and Lark glanced at each other.

"It can't be anything too defiantly Confederate," said Celie. "Clay, do you like the old one about Susan Brown at the dance?"

She and Lark began the verse:

> *Choose your partner as you go,*
> *Choose your partner as you go,*
> *Choose your partner as you go,*
> *Lovely Susan Brown. . . .*

Shadburne and Clay joined in on the chorus:

Fare thee well, my charming girl,
Fare thee well, I'm gone!
Fare thee well, my charming girl,
With golden slippers on!

"And I'll just suit the action to the word," announced Shadburne, rising and taking his broad hat. "Fare thee well, my charming girls, I'm gone. Clay, I'll have my ear cocked for your voice singing that song in Captain Crofut's woods."

"I'll be there," promised Clay, as his friend opened the back door. "I may be there sooner than you think."

❧ 7 ❧

The Charades

The night of Mrs. Parmenter's charades came, calm and bright and mild with its promise of spring at hand. Lark and Clay came early to Mrs. Parmenter's, and found the rooms a bustle of servants and performers.

The double doors had been opened all the way to make one great chamber of parlor and ballroom. Chairs and sofas had been set in rows for the audience. The raised platform was curtained off with dark brocaded draperies to serve as a stage. Along the platform's lip were tallow candles in the tin sconces. To one side were bunched four chairs for the musicians—two fiddles, a flute, and a guitar. Mrs. Parmenter swept and swirled here and there, now as excited as a hen with twice the usual hatching of chickens, now as emphatically authoritative as a brigadier general just promoted for political reasons.

"Lark!" she cried in greeting. "You, too, Lieutenant Buckner—go back of the curtains. Two doors open from other rooms, and I've given them over to the two main charades. Lieutenant Buckner, wait. Lend me that splendid overcoat of yours. Yes, and your sword and your hat."

He gave them to her, and went to join the cast of the "industrial" charade. This was gathered in a small chamber like a study. Most of the people who crowded there were girls and young women, dark and fair, tall and short, stylishly lovely in crinolines and drapes and flounces.

"We're to present our show first," Rowena was announcing. "Come out, all of you, to help set the stage."

Chairs, benches, and the buffet from the parlor for a bar were quickly arranged. On the wall Rowena hung a large white cardboard square, painted in big black capital letters:

ENTERTAINMENT
FOR MAN AND

Below these words appeared a vividly caricatured face, heavy-jowled, squint-eyed, with frowning brows and a drooping mustache.

"I declare, that face is familiar," vowed Constance Cary. "It looks like the pictures of—"

"Of course!" crowed Captain McCarthy. "Benjamin Franklin Butler, the Yankee general yonder on the Peninsula—'Beast' Butler, they nicknamed him at New Orleans!"

"Not so loud, Captain," Rowena warned him. "Let the audience do its own guessing. What about your costumes?"

"I'm ready," announced Mrs. Webb, impressive in

green velvet as the hostess. "But these sleeves are so long. If they could be tucked up—"

"We need pins, and pins are scarce in the Confederacy," mourned Rowena. "Lieutenant Buckner, please step across the hall to Aunt Marianne's music room. I saw half a paper of pins there this morning, fresh from the blockade-runner."

Clay slipped through the curtains, and across the hall to the music room. He turned the knob and opened the door.

A figure in blue whirled around to confront him, a Union officer in gold-braided frock coat and forage cap. For a moment Clay glared, then recognized Major Towers, leaning on his familiar stick.

"What do you want, sir?" demanded the voice of Marianne Parmenter, for once sharp and angry.

She stood beside the piano, Clay's gray overcoat draped upon her shoulders. Papers lay on the top of the piano, weighted down with a dish on which Clay saw a knife and an onion sliced in half.

"I'm sorry," Clay apologized. "I didn't know anybody was here."

"Evidently not," rejoined Mrs. Parmenter. "And why should you come in if nobody was here?"

"Miss Rowena sent me for some pins," Clay stammered in embarrassment.

"Please," Major Towers soothed the lady, "he didn't realize that we were rehearsing. Buckner, please say nothing about our costumes."

"No, we've kept them secret until now," added Mrs.

Parmenter, her fluttery good-humor restored. "You say you want pins? Here, help yourself."

From beside the plate that held the onion she took a folded paper, studded with rows of pins like little picket fences. Clay accepted half a dozen and hurried back to the ballroom.

As he did so, he heard the voices of guests in the hall. A glance showed him the bland smile of Secretary of State Judah P. Benjamin, the handsome face of General Custis Lee, the sterner long-lipped countenance of Secretary of the Navy Mallory, and, behind these two, a tall slim man in a dark coat, with pale fine features and a fringe of chin beard. It was President Jefferson Davis.

Back on the stage he gave the pins to Rowena and donned his grease-spotted apron as bootboy. He pulled off one of his own boots, fitted it carefully over his splinted left arm, and squatted in a corner with a brush to give an impersonation of an industrious polisher. Rowena had pulled a white cap over her elaborate curls and swiftly tied a fluffy apron around her waist, then took two big pewter mugs from Baker's bar.

"We're ready," she declared, and Mrs. Parmenter bustled in through the curtains.

"How the place is filling up," she chattered gaily. "Imagine who just came in—General Stuart, on leave!"

"Let me look," pleaded Constance Cary, and twitched the curtains open by the width of her slim forefinger. Clay, too, peered out.

The rows of chairs were occupied by ladies in party

dresses, men in evening coats and uniforms. Near the double doors to the parlor stood Jeb Stuart, his red-lined cloak draped upon his arm, his plumed hat in his hand. Lark Winstead whispered to him, and he smiled and nodded as though assenting to her words.

Then Mrs. Parmenter waved Constance Cary aside and slid through the curtains to stand before the row of candles that served for footlights. She bubbled cordially with welcome, and reminded the audience that they must contribute generously to the relief fun for which the charades were being offered. Then she explained, as if her guests were a group of little children, what charades were. She predicted that the charades about to be shown would set a thrilling high mark in charade history. Finally:

"We are about to show you the first syllable of the first charade!"

She whisked away audibly. Rowena waved her performers to their places. Squatting again, Clay polished his boot, which already shone like a black mirror. Captain McCarthy slid behind his bar, Rowena posed before it. The curtains opened to a loud and cheerful clapping of hands. Then a chorus of exclamations:

"Look at that sign! Entertainment for man and—what? What's the picture?"

"It's Beast Butler!"

"Entertainment for man and beast—yes—"

"Ha! Ha! Somebody's witty!"

Into view on the stage crowded men and women in traveling coats and hats, laden with carpetbags and umbrellas. One of these was Burton Harrison, the President's secretary. Mrs. Webb, as hostess, made flourishing signs to offer hospitality. The guests sat on the benches or came to the bar, and Rowena rushed here and there with three or four mugs clutched in each slim hand. Burton Harrison bent upon her a gaze of burlesque admiration, caught her elbow, and made as though to kiss her. Dropping one handful of mugs, Rowena slapped his face, and it rang out like a pistol shot. As on signal, the curtains were drawn. More cheers and applause from the audience.

"What a tingler, Miss Rowena!" complained Burton Harrison, rubbing his cheek. "You didn't warn me how hard you can strike."

"All in the spirit of dramatic realism," Rowena laughed at him. "Now all offstage except Colonel Deas and myself."

"The second syllable!" announced Mrs. Parmenter from beyond the curtains.

The sign, the bar, and the benches still proclaimed the inn. Colonel Deas sat at ease, a newspaper open in his hands. In rushed Rowena, capped and aproned still, with broom and dustcloth. She swept furiously around Colonel Deas' chair. He moved his feet and worked his gray brows, but she paid no attention. With the cloth she dusted the chair's back, then flicked at the colonel's immaculate sleeve as though to cleanse flecks of dust from it. The audience burst into laughter as he sprang up in simulated terror and retreated. After him hurried Rowena, her cloth busy at the back of his coat. He sank down, exhausted, on a bench; and with her dust-cloth Rowena roughly mopped his face. At last she stepped back, struck her hands together, and the curtains closed amid a new storm of approval.

"Miss Rowena's most of the show herself," commented Page McCarthy from the side.

"She likes to be most of the show," replied Mary Triplett. "Ready now for the third syllable."

Clay helped McCarthy strip away the sign with Butler's face, and moved the buffet to simulate a judge's desk. The benches were lined up at one side for the jury, and a chair was reversed to serve for the prisoner's dock. Clay stood there, a dark greatcoat over his uniform and massive old shackles on his wrists.

"The third syllable!" Mrs. Parmenter's voice proclaimed, and the curtains pulled back to reveal the trial scene.

Judge Ould presided in a black robe and an immense wig of white yarn. The two attorneys pleaded, first in accusation, then in defense, with melodramatic arm wavings and silent waggings of their jaws. In turn they silently harangued the jury, which filed out and returned at once. The foreman rose and signified a verdict of guilty by turning his thumb down like a Roman Emperor dooming a gladiator.

Clay bowed his head in despair. Judge Ould pointed a finger at him, scowled fearsomely, and condemned him to the gallows by signing a noose about his own throat. Then, suddenly, Rowena was back on stage.

She did not wear her cap and apron now, but appeared in her rich party dresss. She clasped her hands before Judge Ould as though begging mercy, then spun and ran toward Clay and flung herself upon his chained hands.

His sound arm supported her sagging weight as she seemed to swoon. Out of sight, behind Clay's back, her hands clapped; and the curtains were drawn.

"Offstage, everyone!" cried Rowena.

Clay divested himself of shackles and greatcoat, and moved toward the exit from the stage.

"And how did that lovely armful seem to you, Lieutenant?" McCarthy asked him.

"Heavy as a sack of meal," replied Clay honestly, and someone laughed. It was Lark, holding the curtain open for him to emerge at the side of the stage. He went with her to the rear of the auditorium.

Mrs. Parmenter now announced "the whole word," and the curtains opened once more.

Rowena's sewing circle of beauties was displayed, scissors snipping and needles flying. A gray sleeve was finished, another. Rowena, in the middle of the group, held these articles on high for the audience to admire. Everyone huddled close to stitch together the body of the coat. Then Rowena beckoned offstage. Page McCarthy entered in his shirt sleeves. Rowena held out the newly made uniform coat and he put it on, smiling gratefully while the girls made an admiring ring around him. A slap of Rowena's hands and the curtains closed, while the audience burst into a many-voiced argument.

"The first syllable was inn," vowed Judah Benjamin.

"The sign showed that—entertainment for man and Beast Butler."

"And the second syllable had to do with dust," offered Custis Lee.

"Industrial, then," cried out Benjamin. "Because there was a trial for the third syllable, and my heart bled for the poor defendant." He stood up and raised his voice. "Industrial: I suggest that the word was industrial!"

Rowena appeared through the curtains. "That is correct," she said, smiling at the applause. "And now the second charade."

Mrs. Parmenter poked out her head in turn. "It will seem simple after what you have witnessed," she cried. "One scene only, and each syllable appears as a separate word, and all of them together make the whole word, Are you ready? So are we."

Her head vanished. After a moment the parting curtains revealed the oft-used buffet, with a bowl filled with apples, turnips, and ears of corn on it. In stole a blue figure—Major Towers, limping along with his cane in one hand, a sack in the other. Several of the audience hissed at sight of his Federal uniform, and he glanced at them in comic horror, touching a finger to his bearded lips for silence. He approached the buffet and began to take the fruits and cobs, one by one, and drop them into his bag.

"Something about stealing," conjectured a lady near Clay.

Another figure moved into view, and hand clapping

greeted the gray overcoat and broad hat. It was Mrs. Parmenter, dressed in the things she had borrowed from Clay. Her hand wielded the gold-mounted sword, its point prodded Towers' back. He jumped as though in pain and terror, turned to see her, and cowered. Still the sword point menaced him. In a cringing manner, he surrendered the sack of plunder. From it Mrs. Parmenter selected an apple. She bit into it, rolled her fine eyes as though in relish, and took another bite. The curtain closed.

Loudly the ladies and gentlemen cried out their acclaim and mystification:

"What did it mean?"

"The Yankee was stealing and the Confederate lady was eating—"

"Did the apple signify anything?"

"We give up, we yield!"

Out came Mrs. Parmenter, Clay's hat in one hand, the sword in the other.

"Can nobody guess?" she challenged triumphantly. "No? Very well—the word was ingratiate."

"What?" asked a dozen voices together.

"In—gray—she—ate." Mrs. Parmenter spaced the syllables. "Ingratiate. Now the mystery is solved for you."

"Not all of it," said Clay, half-aloud.

"What are you talking about?" asked Lark beside him.

"Not all the mystery," he elaborated. "I was in the music room where they were rehearsing. And there was a plate with an onion cut in two. It didn't appear in their charade."

"An onion cut in two?" repeated Lark. "Clay, I wonder—"

Mrs. Parmenter, still on the stage, held up her hand for attention.

"And now the third charade of the evening!" she announced.

"Oh, I must hurry," said Lark breathlessly. "Clay, wait for me until it's over. Don't go near that onion cut in two, not until I come back."

She raced off toward the stage.

ᕖ 8 ᕗ

Onion Juice

Clay goggled after Lark, and knew that he must look stupid. A hand touched his sleeve, and he looked around to see Rowena's confident smile.

"I venture to think our charade will be voted better than their pilgrimage," she said.

"Pilgrimage," that was Lark's word. Rowena was indiscreet to say it in the hearing of those who would be asked to guess. He frowned at her, but she only smiled again, in amusement and mockery.

The curtains had opened, and a big dark-whiskered man stood by the ever-present buffet, on which he opened a professional-looking black bag.

"That's Mr. John R. Thompson," Rowena told Clay. "The editor, you know. They say he writes such witty verses."

"I know one of his songs," nodded Clay. "About *jine the cavalry—*"

He shut his mouth quickly. He had almost added that he had served as a cavalry scout.

Now appeared two girls, supporting between them a drooping, trembling youth who crinkled his face and clasped his midriff as though in dire pain.

"Theodore De Leon," whispered Rowena, as though making an introduction.

The exaggeratedly sick gentleman fell rather than sat upon a chair. John R. Thompson studied him narrowly, felt his pulse, and with a beckoning finger ordered him to thrust out his tongue for inspection. Then, from the black bag, Thompson produced a round object, bright red and as big as a lemon.

Theodore De Leon stared in sudden horror, lifted his hands to ward off the dose, and then, as Thompson tried to thrust the pill into his mouth, sprang from the chair and fled. Thompson and the two girls pursued him. He ran around the chair twice, sprang acrobatically over the buffet, and tried to burrow into the wall. Captured and flung down, he struggled frantically. But Thompson, the sternest of physicians, set a powerful knee upon De Leon's chest and fairly crammed the pill into his gaping mouth. The curtains drew shut, to shouts of laughter.

"The second syllable!" Mrs. Parmenter announced.

All furniture had been cleared from the stage. A proud figure swaggered into view, with fur-trimmed greatcoat and high hat—John R. Thompson again, the picture of a rich waster. From the other side a woman clad in tattered shawl and kerchief tottered, barely recognizable as the stately Mrs. Semmes. She begged with a trembling outstretched palm. The nabob sneered down at her plight. She knelt before him. He made a sweeping movement of his arm as though to reject her plea. In vain she asked for charity with eloquent gestures. Turning his back upon her, Thompson strutted away, delicately pinching snuff from a jeweled box. Mrs. Semmes collapsed in her rags, and the curtains closed.

"That was grim enough," said Rowena, loudly enough for half the audience to hear.

The final syllable was announced, and the scene was set with two chairs. On them sat an old, old man and an old, old woman. But they were not really old for the man was young Burton Harrison, and the grandmotherly figure at his side, in cap and shawl, was Lark Winstead herself. Their hands touched shakily. The orchestra suddenly began to play, and the tune was "John Anderson, My Jo."

"We were more dramatic than that," purred Rowena.

"At least you were, Miss Rowena," Clay could not help replying, and her smile vanished. Up on stage her aunt's voice rang out:

"The whole word!"

The stage had been arranged to look like a shrine. The buffet stood centered against the rear wall, draped in white and set with candles. Upon it stood a cross. Music began, soft and reverent.

A man entered, then another man, then several women and girls. Burton Harrison wore the blanket and feathers of an Indian chief, and put his tomahawk on the altar. John R. Thompson gave up the snuffbox he had carried in the scene with the beggar woman. Girls put bouquets of flowers on the altar. Theodore De Leon, turbaned and robed like a Moslem, salaamed low and then set a glittering silver casket among the flowers. Each pilgrim left an offering and moved away to stand in a posture of reverence at the far side of the stage.

The music changed. "Dixie," it was playing. A sudden gasp of amazed recognition swept over the audience like a gust of wind as a stalwart figure in gray uniform and gold braid appeared.

"General—Stuart!" Rowena stammered in Clay's ear. "So she asked him—and he actually agreed to be in her charade!"

Then all was silent save for the music as Jeb Stuart strode to the altar. From its sheath he drew his gleaming sword, so often raised to lead charging cavalry, and laid it upon the altar. Then he joined the group beyond, his arms folded, his eyes on the ground.

Two nuns came in, black-robed and white-veiled. They were Lark and Celie Winstead. They lifted their hands as though to consecrate the offerings, and the music changed again, to the "Miserere." The curtains drew together, and there was a moment of hushed silence before the applause began.

Again Mrs. Parmenter hurried before the curtains.

"Can you guess the charade?" she was crying.

"Pilgrimage!" called Rowena from where she stood with Clay, and there were yells of agreement.

"Pilgrimage, of course! That pill John Thompson fired down De Leon's throat—"

"And the beggar scene was grim— Then the couple, full of age—"

Clay gazed with utter disgust at Rowena, who laughed.

"You think I shouldn't have spoken? Why are you so upset at such a small thing?"

"Because it was such a small thing," he told her. "I never saw anything smaller."

"Are you trying to tell me—?"

Unceremoniously he walked away from her. The audience was rising from its rows of seats. Clay saw Jefferson Davis smiling gravely, heard Judah Benjamin telling a joke. The ladies gathered around Jeb Stuart, all complimenting him at once.

"Supper across the hall!" Mrs. Parmenter was fairly whooping, and the company moved that way. Slipping through the crowd, Clay came face to face with Lark.

"The onion," she whispered. "The sliced onion, remember? Let's see what happened to it."

They got into the hall among the others, and found the door of Mrs. Parmenter's music room. Clay turned the knob. It was dark inside, but Clay struck a match and lighted a candle on the desk.

His hat and coat lay across the keyboard, and just beyond was the plate with the onion and the knife. Lark stooped to look closely.

"Quite a lot of juice squeezed out," she said, "and see here."

She pointed to a sheet of white paper, on which lay a pen, with a gleaming uninked point.

"Do you understand, Clay?"

"Yes, I do," he said suddenly. "Onion juice makes a sort of invisible ink."

"We used to write notes with it in school," said Lark, and took up the paper.

"Here," grated a voice from the door. "Give me that!"

Major Towers limped swiftly in, still wearing the blue uniform of his charade performance. "Give me that paper!" he commanded again, trying to snatch it.

Lark retreated around the piano, and Clay stepped quickly between her and Towers. "Why are you so anxious to get a blank piece of paper?" he demanded.

Towers struck at him with the cane. Clay warded off the blow with his sound arm, and seized the cane with his hand. A brief struggle, then Towers twisted the curved handle and the cane sprang apart at the silver ring. The two fell back from each other, Clay holding the hollow shank in his hand. Towers had cleared from inside the cane a lean blade of silver-bright steel.

"If I must—" he said, and lunged at Clay.

Clay parried the thrust with the cane shank that had served to hide the blade. Another lunge, and again Clay beat the point aside. Then Lark was behind Towers.

She had come around the piano, and had caught up the knife from the plate. She shoved it against the major's blue back.

"Drop that sword cane or I'll stab you," she warned, and she sounded as though she meant every word of it.

Major Towers grimaced, then threw down the blade. Clay put his foot on it. The door opened again.

"Lieutenant Buckner!" cried Custis Lee.

"We have your spy, General," said Clay. "Major Towers, if that's his name—"

"It's my name," said Towers, his voice completely calm. "Gentlemen, may I remind you that I wear the uniform of a Federal officer, and that I'm entitled to be treated as a prisoner of war, not as a spy. If you want to see further credentials, I have them here."

He put his hand inside the blue coat, but Clay struck his wrist with the shank of cane.

"Don't move!" he warned, then dropped the shank and reached into Towers' inner pocket. He found a pistol and drew it forth.

"This proves it," he said to Custis Lee. "He was going to try to shoot his way free."

Lark was back at the piano, holding the paper close to the flame of the candle. Everyone watched—Custis Lee, Clay, and Towers. Rusty-looking script appeared on the sheet, and Custis Lee took it.

"It's a list of new regiments and at what points they will re-enforce our line below the Rapidan," he reported. "Where did you learn these things, Major Towers, and how were you going to send them to your friends?"

Towers smiled harshly. "Since these two young people have guessed so much and so cleverly, let them guess how I got the information and how I was going to send it."

"I can answer the last question, General," said Clay. "A dollar and a half in Federal money can get a letter carried through our lines to anybody in the North. As to where he learned the news about our troops—"

A tall, gold-braided officer with a pointed tuft of beard was at the door.

"General Young, find a couple of men to guard this prisoner," said Custis Lee. "Be quiet about it, don't excite the other guests."

Young was gone, and someone else came in. It was Mrs. Parmenter, all crinolines and elaborate curls and wide eyes. Behind her came Rowena.

"May I ask what—" she began, then fell silent. She looked at Towers standing against the wall, and at the pistol in Clay's hand.

"There's a mystery here, Mrs. Parmenter," Custis Lee told her. "Look at the writing on this paper. Have you ever seen it before?"

She gave it a quick glance. "Never," she vowed.

"Don't say such a thing, Aunt Marianne," said Rowena tonelessly.

Mrs. Parmenter gazed at her niece. "What are you thinking, child?"

"It's your handwriting," Rowena said.

"Why—but—"

"I can swear to my aunt's handwriting," Rowena assured Custis Lee. "If she's a spy for the Union, then—"

Silence again. Rowena smiled tremulously at Clay.

"You think I love to be in theatricals, Lieutenant Buckner. This is one scene I wish I didn't have to play. But I can't have General Custis Lee think that all our family is false to the South. I am ready to testify that my aunt wrote those words."

Abruptly she hurried out of the room.

"Well," said Mrs. Parmenter, almost brightly, "that makes it foolish for me to try to deny anything, doesn't it?"

General Young returned with Captain McCarthy and another man. At a word from Custis Lee they took charge of Major Towers.

"Take him out by the back way," directed Custis Lee, "and see that he's locked up at the provost marshal's office."

"And I'm under arrest, too," said Mrs. Parmenter, watching Towers depart between his two guards. Her earlier fluttering manner had entirely departed. "General, you and I have been friends in the past. May I ask one favor?"

"If I can grant it."

"I would like to see this evening to its end, as hostess for these guests." She took Custis Lee's arm. "You can keep close to me, General, and see that I don't make a sudden break for freedom."

"Sir," said Clay, "let me ask a favor, too."

Lee faced him. "Anything, Lieutenant Buckner."

"My duty's done here," Clay reminded him. "I want to start back to the front now. Tonight."

"Your arm's still in splints," protested Lark.

"It's ready to be sent back to active duty," Clay insisted. "I can ask the first surgeon I meet to take the splints off. General Lee, I promise to see that your sword and this uniform are brought safely back to your headquarters."

Custis Lee smiled from where he stood, beside the taut-faced Mrs. Parmenter. "I had begun to hope," he said, "that you might like to continue your assignment on my staff. I can promise that your commission will be permanent."

Clay shook his head. "Thank you, General, but the Iron Scouts are looking for me. I've neglected my work with them long enough. I'd like to leave, and at once."

"Very well, then," granted Custis Lee. "I've been grateful for your help, Buckner. Come, Mrs. Parmenter."

Gracefully he escorted her out of the music room. Standing together, Clay and Lark heard her laughing with guests in the hall.

"Let's both go back home now, Clay," said Lark softly. "I certainly don't want to stay in this house and play a gay society part any more. And I do want to be with you until you're ready to leave."

They went out to find a carriage. Neither looked or acted like the triumphant discoverer of enemy spies. But they felt warmly grateful that they could be together.

Night had fallen again as Clay rode Cherokee among dense thickets on Crofut's land above the Rappahannock. The darkness was chill and foggy. He began to sing:

Fare thee well, my charming girl,
Fare thee well, I'm gone. . . .

"You sound like a night hawk with a sore throat," a familiar voice broke in, and Shake Harris rode out of a clump of trees toward him. "Welcome back to trouble, boy."

Hugh Scott appeared at Clay's other stirrup, leaned from his saddle to shake hands warmly, then rode ahead to show the way to camp. They emerged in a clearing where brush shelters masked a small fire. Shadburne rose from where he sat, an arm flung up in greeting. Clay dismounted and loosened Cherokee's saddle girth.

"Did you finish what you were up to in Richmond?" inquired Shadburne.

"I helped dig a couple of spies out of their holes in Richmond," said Clay.

"Congratulations," applauded Hugh Scott, but Clay shook his head.

"It didn't make me happy. The fact is, I was right sorry for both of them. Maybe because they were trying to do for their side what we do for ours."

"But they didn't do it as well," suggested Shake Harris.

"Let's just say they weren't as lucky as we've been," amended Clay. "Where can I tie Cherokee up, and is there any grain for him to eat?"

❧ 9 ❧

The Edge of Battle

The Iron Scouts were frantically busy all that spring of 1864, and afterward Clay found his memories of events so mixed up that he was not sure which incident followed which.

Most of March and April they operated from their camp in the thick woods behind Crofut's farm, venturing by night and by day into the Federal lines. Once Clay, with Shadburne and Jim Sloan, donned blue caps and jackets and rode boldly to the headquarters of the enemy cavalry, across the Rappahannock River from Fredericksburg. They stood at salute while General Sheridan, Grant's new chief of cavalry, walked almost within arm's length of them. He was small and sturdy, with pointed mustaches and slanting eyes.

"Tell that infantry brigadier he can't keep his mounted guards of honor," Sheridan was instructing a staff officer. "I was put in command of all the cavalry, and I'm certainly going to have all of it."

"Sheridan talks like a man who knows his business," observed Clay, as they stole away from the camp.

"He does know his business," Jim Sloan said emphatically. "Everywhere I looked in those lines, the men were busy grooming or watering or feeding their horses. That means Sheridan has a special interest in how his men ride, and they're apt to go into action pretty well in shape."

"What bothers me most is what he said about getting all the cavalry together," Shadburne added his word. "The Federals have always had more cavalry than we have, but they've kept it scattered out—a squadron here, a regiment there—for headquarters guards or courier duty. I don't want to see Jeb Stuart hit with twice his number of men and horses."

"Don't worry about old Jeb," Clay said confidently. "He always manages to have more men than the other side at whatever point the fighting breaks out."

"What will Ulysses S. Grant be like, at the head of all those Yanks?" wondered Jack Shoolbred.

A partial answer to that question came in the form of a general order to the blue Army of the Potomac which Jud Prioleau brought back from a stealthy visit to a divisional headquarters. It directed that all sutlers with the Federal forces everywhere depart by April 16, on pain of having their wagons and stocks of delicacies confiscated.

"I see General Meade's signature on it," said Prioleau, "but it's Grant talking. He wants his army to live hard and fight hard."

"And isn't it a mean trick to play on us?" demanded Hugh Scott. "I don't want to be the one to carry this piece of news back to our lines. The main reason our boys want another battle is that they hope to capture a few sutler wagons and fill up on cake and pickles and things like that."

"I wonder if Sheridan has heard of the Iron Scouts yet," mused Shadburne.

Sheridan had heard of them, as the Iron Scouts learned when Dick Hogan stole a mail pouch from a blue-jacketed courier at a crossroads tavern. It contained a letter from Sheridan to Major General Christopher C. Augur in Washington:

> I have 100 men who will take the contract to clean out Shadburne's gang of Iron Scouts. I want 100 Spencer rifles for them. Send them to me if they can be found in Washington.

"Spencer rifles," read Shake Harris aloud. "Aren't those the repeating kind?"

"Sure enough," Barney Hennegan told him. "You can load a Spencer on Monday and fire it off all week. That means just so much more dodging for all of us."

"If they've picked a hundred men to hunt us, we'll have to hunt the hundred men," announced Shadburne. "I want to find out the name of the chief of that bunch of scouts, and where they're camped." His heavily bearded face creased in a frown. "Right now they seem to know more about us than we do about them."

"They know your name, George," agreed Hogan, "and we don't know who's their chief."

"But we know there's an even hundred of them,"

growled Bob Dulin, the self-appointed avenger of blood. "Right now, that is. Maybe we can reduce that hundred here and there in the near future. They don't know how many we are."

"Or how few," added Prioleau. "Anyway, it's a kind of compliment, telling off a hundred picked men to try to clean us out."

"When it comes to that, we don't even know what Ulysses S. Grant looks like," put in Hugh Scott. "All we know is that big list of battles he won out west. I reckon on him being about seven feet tall, with fiery red whiskers and powder smoke curling out of his nose."

But Jim Sloan visited Culpeper in blue uniform, and disappointed Scott with the word he brought back of Grant's appearance. The new Federal chieftain was described as of small stature, with a close-cropped beard and a shabbier uniform than anyone on his staff.

"He smokes cigars every minute," elaborated Sloan. "If we could cut off his tobacco, we might win this war yet."

Night after night one or another of the Iron Scouts slipped across the Rapidan with what news his comrades had gathered. On April 27, Shadburne learned that the latest re-enforcements demanded by Grant, the twenty thousand men of the hard-bitten Ninth Army Corps under General Ambrose Burnside, had left Maryland for the front. Another important bit of information was picked up on April 30—Grant would move with the whole Army of the Potomac on May 4. On the following day, deep in the South, Sherman would strike at the Confederates defending Atlanta. And on May 6, Butler's thirty thousand troops on the Virginia Peninsula would assail forts to the south of Richmond and seek to destroy railroad lines that supplied the Confederate capital.

Clay carried that last budget of information, swimming Cherokee across the Rapidan to reach one of Stuart's reserve posts.

"This is right interesting and right helpful," said the officer who received the report. "All we need to know now is where Grant will throw that nation of bluecoats—at our right or our left or maybe into our center."

Not until the day of the movement itself could the Iron Scouts supply that definite information. On the bright morning of May 4, the whole landscape above the Rapidan seemed to swarm with blue legions, marching for Germanna Ford. Shadburne, Clay, and half a dozen others mounted and floundered across the river with the news. Gray troops went into motion to meet the Federals. The two armies did not strike each other that day, but on the foggy morning of the fifth they drew together.

Clay was scouting on the edge of the battle that followed. The trees of the Virginia Wilderness, bright green with spring foliage, obscured a view of the fighting; but the air seemed ripped to shreds by the incessant gunfire. To Clay the volleys of musketry sounded like a thousand axes frantically chopping, and the repeated louder booms of cannon, like great trees crashing to earth. Clay and his friends rode their horses into a lather, spying out the movements of the enemy left flank that seemed to force itself eastward and ever eastward.

The sun went down with that enemy flank movement halted and contained. Grant's advance had not been driven back, but it had been stopped. The Iron Scouts camped with Jeb Stuart's picket line at the right of where the Army of Northern Virginia lay down on its arms in the face of the Federals among the trees opposite.

Weary as they were, Shadburne and his friends spent a full hour grooming and comforting their overworked horses by firelight. Clay spread his own blanket over Cherokee and fetched water in the crown of his hat for lack of a pail. Afterward he watched as Cherokee munched early grass and ate a few handfuls of corn from a saddlebag.

"You must have ridden that nag hard all day," commented a Virginia colonel, strolling near. "How will he carry you tomorrow?"

"He'll do his best, sir," replied Clay.

"Suppose you spare him tomorrow's work," the colonel went on, "because there'll be more fighting tomorrow, you know."

"I know, and both Cherokee and I will be needed," replied Clay. "No rest for either of us tomorrow."

"I happen to have four fine horses," the colonel told him. "Three of them are fresh and ready. Let me take that poor jaded fellow, and I'll give you your pick of the three and two hundred Confederate dollars to boot."

"Thank you, no, sir," Clay fairly snapped. "Cherokee and I know how to get along together."

"Sorry you won't trade. Good luck, then." And the colonel walked away.

Clay woke before dawn to hear the guns booming again. He was glad to see Cherokee much improved by a night's rest, and quickly saddled him. The Iron Scouts munched hard crackers as they rode out to see where the battle would be.

Grant was moving eastward again, and the smaller Confederate army strained to keep pace with him and block his way to Richmond. That was the story of the day of May 6, and of the next day, and the next, with the deafening rattle-roar of guns and the struggling clouds of smoke from exploded powder and blazing trees. Men seemed to fall by squads and regiments, generals dying as well as privates. Clay, speeding here and there on his missions, saw great trains of ambulances bearing away enough wounded men to cram a whole city of hospitals. Back and forth raged the fighting in the Wilderness, but steadily the mighty army of Grant nosed its way eastward, trying to find a route around the right flank of Lee.

Stuart's cavalry dismounted again and again to fight on foot against Federal infantry, then mounted swiftly to head off cavalry.

"Doesn't this man Grant know when he's been whipped?" demanded a Georgia sergeant of Clay during a lull between volleys. "Up to now, whenever we set back a Yankee general—McClellan, Burnside, Hooker—he pulled away to patch himself up. Grant just keeps on coming."

Sheridan kept coming, too. On May 9, Bill Mikler galloped in to say that a great force of mounted Federals —they made a line thirteen miles long, and must number more than ten thousand—had wriggled past the Confederate right and was heading southward on the Telegraph Road toward Richmond.

Every available gray cavalryman went with Stuart to pursue, but the Iron Scouts stayed to observe the further moves of Grant's main army. They were able to diagnose and report the advance of a column toward Spotsylvania Court House, and infantry of the Second Corps of the Army of Northern Virginia toiled to throw up breastworks among groves and fields to protect the position. Then came more battle, three days of it, deafening and sickening.

The Iron Scouts served both as pickets and couriers, and they saw the most desperate conflict any of them could remember. Several times the stubborn Federals charged to the very defenses, and had to be driven back with bayonets and rifle butts. Rain fell, but did not dampen the deadly determination of either army. So many were killed and wounded behind the muddy earthen defenses of the Confederates that companies dwindled down to mere squads, and regiments became as small as companies.

When, on May 13, the Federals sagged back at last from that grim series of grappling assaults, Shadburne led his companions eastward again, to look for evidence of a possible new flanking movement. Clay, riding at point for the party along a narrow woodland path, came face to face with a Union cavalryman and pointed a revolver at him. "You're my prisoner," Clay announced.

The fellow was stocky, with sandy stubble on his square face. "Just drop that gun, Johnny Reb, and see how quick I knock you bowlegged with my fists," he challenged.

"Pick on somebody your size," growled huge Barney Hennegan, cantering up beside Clay. The Federal stared, then shrugged and grinned.

"Shucks," he said, "there ain't anybody my size here. This rebel with the hand gun is about half as big as I am, and you're twice as big. So let's drop the subject of fist fighting."

Shadburne joined them and caught the man's bridle. "Where are you from, Yank?"

"Down close to Richmond," was the reply.

"You were on that raid of Sheridan's?" asked Shadburne. "Jeb Stuart must have chased you back quicker than you went down."

"Jeb Stuart's through chasing anybody."

Hennegan's huge hand prowled in a saddlebag. "This man's a courier with messages," he announced. "Here's something addressed to Federal headquarters."

Shadburne tore open the envelope and pulled out the letter. His eyes widened and his face grew pale.

"This is a lie," he snapped out.

"Not if it says Jeb Stuart got killed," said the prisoner. "A boy in one of the Michigan regiments shot him just before we turned back."

The Iron Scouts looked at each other wretchedly.

"It can't be," mumbled Clay. "I saw him in Richmond—"

He remembered Jeb Stuart, laughing gallantly with Lark, striding like a hero across the stage in the charade. As Clay shook his head in amazed unbelief, rain fell wearily through the branches above them.

≫ 10 ≪

The Hundred Picked Men

Clay had taken the revolver from the holster at the prisoner's waist belt, and Hennegan possessed himself of a saber that looked like a toy in the giant's immense hand. From a sheath on the saddle Shadburne dragged forth a short-barreled, well-kept rifle.

"A Spencer, by all that's holy!" Shadburne cried. "Spencers were mighty scarce just a few days back, according to what I saw in a letter your General Sheridan wrote. In fact, he was hard pushed to get Spencers for a certain hundred picked men."

"What are you jabbering about?" asked the stocky Federal, with a fine show of carelessness.

"Who's your commander?" Shadburne snapped at him.

"Why, Ulysses S. Grant's my commander. Even a rebel knows that."

"Your captain, I mean."

"Don't serve under no captain."

The rain began to fall harder—or was it the drumming of hoofs?

"Look out!" warned Clay suddenly, and fired the captured revolver at blue riders coming down the trail toward them.

That cry galvanized every Iron Scout into action. Shadburne, Scott, Shake Harris, and Bob Dulin all drew and fired their own pistols, so swiftly that the noise was like a multiple echo of Clay's shot. The enemy's sudden rush stopped, and then the Iron Scouts fled back the way they had come, hustling the prisoner along in their midst.

They came out into an open field, wallowed across a stream beyond, and into brush on its far bank. At once Shadburne flung up his hand for a halt.

"We'll make our stand here," he said. "No point in running from one bunch into the arms of another. Dismount."

They did so. Shadburne's eye flicked around.

"Eight," he counted. "Harris, Hennegan, lead the horses back, and take the prisoner with you. Take cover, the rest of you. When they come, wait for my word. Give them a volley if they rush, and reload quickly. Keep your revolvers for close quarters."

The six of them crouched behind trees, logs, in low places of the brushy ground, their long gun barrels shoved to the fore. Clay felt rain trickling down his collar. On one side of him was Hugh Scott, on the other side Bob Dulin. Jim Sloan and Jud Prioleau knelt a little distance beyond Dulin. Shadbourne stood erect, peering across the stream and the open ground beyond.

"Here they come!" He crawled out, and fired with his rifled musket.

The pursuers had begun to appear out of the woods on the far side of the field, but at the report of Shadburne's gun they paused and melted back among the trees.

"Better stay away!" howled Shadburne at the top of his lungs. "Your Spencers can shoot faster, but our muzzle-loaders can hit harder and farther away!"

A man on a black horse, in the forefront of the blue vanguard, swept his arms in quick gestures to motion his companions back.

"Take cover! Take cover!" this man bawled.

"I know him," snarled Dulin, and fired.

The black horse leaped violently, as though hit, and dashed away up the trail again. The others vanished after it.

"That was Tryon," said Dulin, swiftly ramming down another charge. "Remember him?"

Tryon. . . . Clay remembered him most vividly. That was the name of the man who had tried again and again to hunt out the Iron Scouts, who had played hide-and-seek with Clay in Richmond all the early summer of 1863, who at times had seemed almost friendly, almost brotherly, in his gallant give-and-take of scouting warfare. Now he was over there, leading those hundred horsemen with repeating rifles.

"Wish I'd hit him where he was biggest, instead of just nicking his horse," Dulin was saying.

"No more shooting!" Shadburne warned. "If they come out into the open again, wait until I give the word. Then three of you—Buckner, Scott, Prioleau—each try to hit his target. The rest of us will wait for a rush."

But the Federals still lurked among the trees. They began to blaze away from between the trunks. The Iron Scouts waited in silence, while bullets whipped and droned through the summer foliage above them.

"Here they come," warned Dulin, his rifle going to his shoulder.

"No, just one man, waving a flag of truce," said Clay quickly.

The bluecoat moved forward on foot into the open field. Above his head he flourished a white cloth. Shadburne raised his voice:

"All right, Yankee, come along by yourself and we won't fire! Do you want to surrender?"

"That sounds like Sergeant George Shadburne!" whooped back the other. "I was going to ask you the same question, Shadburne!"

"It's Tryon, all right," said Clay.

Tryon wore blue cavalry uniform, with gold emblems on his shoulders. He came confidently close to the brink of the stream.

"Good day to you, Iron Scouts," he called, his voice as friendly as though they were playing a game at a picnic. "There's a hundred of us strung out here, and if you try to run again we'll gobble you up. Why don't you just consider the war's over as far as you're concerned, and come back with me? We've got mighty good coffee, and sardines and canned peaches for supper."

"Well, well, Tryon!" cried Shadburne, equally genial

in his hiding. "So you're captain of the hundred men who took the contract to wipe us out!"

"Not captain. I'm a major now. How did you know about us?"

"We've been reading Sheridan's mail. But what makes you think you've got us outnumbered?"

"Because you aren't trying to fight back," replied Tryon. "I know you well enough to know that, if you were anywhere near our numbers, you'd be counterattacking instead of swapping friendly talk. Where's my old friend, Clay Buckner?"

"Where you don't expect to find him," Shadburne replied. "Wherever you don't see Iron Scouts, there's where we're the thickest. And any moment our flanking party's going to mop you up. Better pull out of here while there's still something like a hundred of you."

"You wouldn't warn me about a flanking party if you had one," laughed Tryon. "Well, if you won't listen to reason, I'll stop arguing."

He shrugged, turned on his heel, and marched toward the woods where his men waited. He moved with careless confidence, as if scornful of the guns behind him. As he approached the trees, he raised his voice.

"Open fire! Fill that brush full of lead!"

Dozens of shots barked out. The air seemed to pop and quiver with the incessant fire of the repeaters. Clay threw himself flat as bullets hummed over him like murderous bees.

"Look out for a rush," warned Shadburne. "Ready to fire when I give the word."

The enemy fusillade did not slacken as, to either side of the woods, blue forms stole into view.

"They're going to charge us," Clay heard Hugh Scott say.

Just then a wild whoop rang from the right. Into view, across the stream and into the field, rushed a huge mounted figure—Barney Hennegan. He waved his captured saber, fired a pistol, and yelled back over his shoulder.

"Hit this flank, men!" his voice rang stridently. "The other squadron will take them in the rear!"

Louder than the gunfire, heavy crashing sounded in the bushes.

"Rebel cavalry!" screamed a Federal, and ran for cover. So did his neighbor. So did others. At Shadburne's word, the Iron Scouts fired their rifles and, as the noise of hoofs and breaking branches seemed to fill the whole world, the enemy advance melted back into the trees from which it had come.

"Get them!" Shadburne was roaring. "Before they reach their horses—cut them off!"

"Stand and fight, boys!" Clay heard the distant cry of Tryon. "It's only a trick!"

But the repeaters crackled no more. Those hundred picked men had taken flight. Hennegan reined around and galloped in among his dismounted friends.

"Quick, let's go," he panted. "That prisoner got away, and he'll tell his friends how few we really are."

"How did you make it sound like a whole regiment?" demanded Scott.

"Harris got the horses in among some fire-killed bushes, and whipped them back and forth to break the twigs and branches. Here he comes now."

They mounted and raced off through a new spatter of rain. At a crossroads they swung to the right, found a pass between two low hills, and hurried on toward the nearest position of Confederate infantry.

"I still wish I'd shot that Tryon," snorted Dulin, riding close to Clay.

"I'm glad you didn't," said Clay quickly.

And he realized that he was glad. If hatred of the enemy was a good soldier's duty, Clay knew that he must make exception where Tryon was concerned. Tryon did his best for the right as he saw it, even as Clay did. He hoped that he and Tryon would be spared to the end of the war, and might meet and shake hands like friends.

Back at cavalry headquarters, they sadly heard confirmation of the report of Jeb Stuart's death, but there was no time to mourn.

The cavalry did its share of the fighting that went on in the Wilderness day after day. Wade Hampton fairly raced up from South Carolina, a fresh brigade of horsemen behind him, to command where Stuart had fallen.

Hampton, huge, quiet, and sober-faced, was a vastly different cavalry leader from Stuart. Almost at once his regiments found themselves being told again and again to dismount and fight with muskets like infantry. They turned back a Federal column at Hawes Shop, and another on the flank at the Battle of Cold Harbor.

Some of the Iron Scouts fought in these actions, but not Clay. He, Scott, and one or two others kept busy behind the Federal lines, eyes and ears alert for information of fresh threatening moves.

It was on June 7 that Clay and Scott, perched high on a bluff above New Castle on the Pamunkey, watched in amazement the spectacle of long columns of mounted Federals crossing, not southward toward the fighting, but northward away from it.

"That looks like a good share of what cavalry Sheridan has," growled Scott. "What are they running away from? We're not after them. How many are there, Clay?"

"I'm counting their flags," replied Clay, pushing his face between tussocks of grass at the very lip of the bluff. "Let's see. Twelve—thirteen—I make it fifteen regimental flags. Call it six hundred men at least to each regiment, and that makes nine thousand officers and troopers."

"With four batteries," added Scott. "Sixteen to twenty guns. And all of them going fast away from trouble."

"More likely going a roundabout way to look for trouble," amended Clay. "All right, what do we do next?"

"You and I split up. Your Cherokee's a lot faster than my horse, so race him back to headquarters. Tell General Hampton what we saw, and say that I'll be along pretty quick with more information about which way this bunch of Yankees is pointing its nose."

It was a ride of only a dozen miles to where the cavalry lay camped above Richmond, near the scene of the surprise of Kilpatrick's raiders three months earlier. General Hampton came out of the half-ruined cabin where he maintained headquarters and listened to Clay's report. His brigadiers joined him as Clay talked. Clay recognized them, three tall, beard-tufted young men—Calbraith Butler, Tom Rosser, and Pierce Young, who had helped arrest Towers in Mrs. Parmenter's music room.

"This double-back maneuver of Sheridan's isn't as mysterious as it sounds to you all," commented Hampton when Clay had finished. "The dispatches say that there's a strong enemy advance along the Shenandoah Valley toward Lynchburg. That cavalry may be heading along to join in the fun."

"Lynchburg," repeated Butler. "But if they moved northward across the Pamunkey they can't get at Lynchburg unless they turn around and come back across the North Anna farther upstream."

"Which means we'll slide along this side of the North Anna and wait for them," replied Hampton drily. "Gentlemen, get your commands in shape to march, but tell nobody where or why. We'll hang on here until tomorrow morning, in the hope that Scott rides in with more news." He turned back to Clay. "Get yourself some rest, Buckner, and tell Shadburne that whatever hour Scott arrives—morning, night, or noon—to send him to me at once."

Scott was in camp early the following afternoon. He

told his story, first to Hampton, then to Shadburne and the other Iron Scouts. The Federal cavalry was led by Sheridan in person, numbered fully ten thousand, and had begun to head westward before Scott had ridden away. Big wagons, laden with pontoons for the crossing of rivers, rolled along with Sheridan.

"Ten thousand men," summed up Shadburne. "We have maybe six thousand fit to ride, maybe fewer than that."

"And no Jeb Stuart to lead us," mourned Dulin, oiling his big revolver.

"Old Wade Hampton's no Jeb Stuart, but he's a purely poisonous fighting man," volunteered Hugh Scott. "He gets in close to his work."

"No closer than Jeb did," insisted Dulin loyally.

"I'm not taking anything away from Jeb Stuart, and I wish he was alive and well and here with us," rejoined Scott, "but you've got to give it to Old Wade. He's good on your side in a fuss. He's one of the best shots in the army, and he can cut you in two with that long old sword of his."

"I declare this debating society adjourned," spoke up Shadburne. "Get what sleep you can, all of you. I reckon we'll be riding before sunup."

Before they lay down, quartermasters came to distribute rations—a pound and a half of hardtack and eight ounces of bacon per man. Shadburne told his companions to fill sacks with corn, as much as could ride comfortably at a saddlebow. By daybreak of June 9, they were off to the westward.

The Iron Scouts rode on the right flank of the column, between the troops and the North Anna, peering at every crossing. The day was hot, bright, and dusty. But Hampton kept his men moving, with but brief rests, all that day and most of the night. They bivouacked the evening of June 10 among pleasant meadows and groves at Trevilian Station on the Virginia Central Railway, while Clay and the other scouts watched Sheridan's force make its way by pontoon bridge across the North Anna River. Rested and ready, Hampton's cavalry met and fought Sheridan's in the morning, and Sheridan fell back the way he had come.

Clay took no part in the main fighting, but helped with the pursuit and harrying of Sheridan's retreat. He and Shake Harris came upon a Federal the third day after the fight, dismounted and leading his worn-out horse. The man had a Spencer repeater on his saddle, like the hundred picked men under Tryon they had skirmished with in May.

"How's Major Tryon?" asked Harris, pointing his pistol.

The prisoner squinted up at them. "You know the major?"

"He and I are friends, sort of," Clay informed him. "Did he get through the fight at Trevilian Station all right?"

"He was promoted and transferred before we started out," said the Federal. "He's Lieutenant Colonel Tryon now."

"And who's commanding your gang of Iron Scout hunters?" inquired Harris.

"You know so much about us, don't you know we've been cut up into small patrols? We don't care about the Iron Scouts any more."

"Why not?"

"Grant quit fighting above Richmond. He slid clear around below Petersburg, and he's got Lee bottled up in the trenches there. Your Iron Scouts aren't the bother they used to be."

≫ 11 ≪
Walking Rations

The prisoner had told the truth. The Army of Northern Virginia had had to hurry headlong to meet Grant's new threat against the Petersburg defenses, twenty miles below the Confederate capital. Now the fighting was done in trenches and behind fortifications hastily dug by both armies. Hampton's cavalry found itself strung along either side of the Weldon Railroad that ran south of Petersburg to bring up supplies from North Carolina and the Deep South.

"We'll have to change our base of operations, too," declared Shadburne. "Come on, Iron Scouts, we'll show them whether we aren't the bother we used to be."

Before the Federals had drawn their ramparted lines clear and strong around Petersburg, Shadburne led his men deep into Blackwater Swamp, to the west of the new battleground. This territory was a dank and almost tropical expanse of trees, heavily bearded with vines and so crisscrossed with soggy, muddy streams that it was slow and dangerous work to travel through it without a full knowledge of the winding trails over occasional solid ground.

Deep in the heart of Blackwater Swamp, at the very source of Blackwater River, the Iron Scouts set up their camp, a huddle of low-built shelters well masked in vines and bushes, with great screens of closely twined vegetation to hide their fires at night. From that base they learned the way toward Federal headquarters at City Point, no more than a dozen miles away on the James River. Creeping close, they spied out troop movements. Heavy Union forces lay between them and the Confederate defenses around Petersburg and Richmond, but they slipped away to southward and carried information to Wade Hampton and Calbraith Butler, on guard along the Weldon Railroad.

July and August were steamy hot in Blackwater Swamp, and hotter than that in the Petersburg trenches where Lee's reduced army staved off the determined thrusts of more than twice its numbers. After several skirmishes with Hampton, little General Sheridan was transferred. The Iron Scouts learned that he was being hurried away to the Shenandoah Valley, from which mountain-girt stronghold the bitterly audacious Jubal Early threatened an attack on Washington itself. But most of Sheridan's cavalry remained near Petersburg, and it was harder to fight than ever.

Late in August, the Iron Scouts were able to expose a movement of Federals near Reams Station that threatened the indispensable Weldon Railroad. Cavalry and infantry repulsed that force, and to Shadburne in

Blackwater Swamp came a letter of praise and thanks in the handwriting of Robert E. Lee himself. Shadburne read the letter aloud in the vine-masked camp on the last hot day of August. Clay and Hennegan boiled pork fryings and the ashes of oak and hickory bark to make soap for themselves and their comrades. The others cleaned weapons or mended clothing as they listened.

"I understand that the Yanks have stopped their raids for the time being," said Shadburne, when he had finished reading the dispatch. "Now would be our time to raid, the way old Jeb Stuart used to ride here and there and make everybody wonder what he was up to. But where? And what after?"

"Food," replied Shake Harris. "We're not doing so bad ourselves, out here away from all the foraging parties. But I hear tell the boys are right hungry around Petersburg. I've got a cousin in the infantry who says they're lucky to get a bite of corn pone and four ounces of bacon a day. That's not my notion of grub enough to do any fighting on."

"We couldn't carry back enough rations to help the army any," objected Jud Prioleau, taking a blazing twig from under the soap kettle to light his pipe. "We'd need rations that could walk themselves—"

"Walking rations!" interrupted Clay. "I know what that means."

"Hush your foolishness," grunted Hennegan, "and help me trickle cold water in to set this mess of soap. It'll make us enough to wash everybody's neck and ears all week."

"Major Towers told the yarn—Major Towers, the spy I helped catch in Richmond," elaborated Clay. "He claimed to be a Confederate officer who marched a big herd of cattle clear across country from beyond the Mississippi—"

"He was lying, wasn't he?" said Prioleau.

"Yes, but it could happen. A herd of walking, moving cattle—"

"You mean that Yankee cattle herd at Coggin's Point," put in Hugh Scott. "Three thousand beef you and I figured it to be when we scouted close there a week ago. Big steers, too. They'd butcher out at eight hundred pounds each."

"How much is eight hundred times three thousand?" inquired Prioleau.

"Two million four hundred thousand pounds," calculated Shadburne at once. "At a pound a day, that would feed Marse Robert's fifty thousand men for better than forty days and forty nights."

"But the Union Army doesn't let that many cattle run around loose for the taking," Prioleau objected.

"What if we slip in while they're looking somewhere else?" said Shadburne. "Clay has a real idea. Finished with that soap boiling? All right, let's ride out and have a good look at just how well they've got their cattle guard up."

Half a dozen went with Shadburne on the expedition. They slipped cautiously through the dense mud-rooted woods to a spot just opposite the heavily garrisoned defenses of Grant's headquarters at City Point.

Narrowly they observed the camps and dispositions of thousands of troops, as well as the shipping in the James River beyond to the east. Then they slipped downstream, fully five miles.

"Hark!" said Shadburne. "I hear cattle bawling."

Sure enough, distant bellows sounded.

"Scott and Prioleau, go make sure what the situation is," ordered Shadburne.

The two stole away, and came back in an hour. Great rough pens lay strung along the riverbank at Coggin's Point, and perhaps a hundred and twenty men were on duty there. Most of these were unarmed civilians. The cattle numbered about three thousand, as Clay and Scott had earlier guessed.

"That would be a big run of steers, even back at my home in Texas," said Shadburne. "If those cattle tenders are unarmed, where's the nearest military post?"

More scouting revealed that a whole mounted regiment lay in the woods two miles upstream toward City Point. Shadburne himself poked close enough to find that this was the First District of Columbia Cavalry.

"And no big force any nearer," he said. "They don't imagine any danger to all those steaks and roasts. Give me some paper and a pencil. I'll write a note to General Hampton."

Harris bore Shadburne's message away, and the others returned to camp. They were washing their clothes with the homemade soap when Harris returned at sundown, carrying a message. Shadburne read it and grimaced in his beard.

"Hark to what Old Wade wants us to find out next," he said. "He says, 'Tell me when Grant will visit Washington, or Sheridan in the Valley.' All right, is anybody here friendly enough with Ulysses S. Grant to give us his travel plans?"

Nobody could give an answer, then or for three days afterward. Then some of the scouts waylaid a courier, and in the captured letter pouch found an order saying that Grant would leave on September 14 for a conference with Sheridan in the Shenandoah Valley. That news went to Hampton's headquarters south of Petersburg, and back came orders for Shadburne to bring his men into the cavalry camp by the evening of September 13. Next morning at sunrise, Hampton was on the move.

He had chosen twenty-six hundred men whose horses were in condition to stand several days and nights of hard marching. Four cannon rolled along with these riders. Hampton's lieutenants were huge Rooney Lee, Robert E. Lee's son, and Tom Rosser. The direction of the day's march was southward instead of northward, along the bank of a tree-fringed little stream called Rowanty Creek. Even Shadburne was mystified, but no Federal troops showed anywhere that day. The riders forded the creek after sundown and camped with their faces northward again.

"Scout ahead of us, Shadburne," Clay heard Hampton say as they resumed their march in the gray dawn. "Take the road to Cook's Bridge on the Blackwater River, right where it flows out of that sticky swamp you and your scouts inhabit."

"Cook's Bridge, sir?" echoed Shadburne. "But the Federals tore that bridge down a month ago."

"I know that," Hampton told him. "Ride ahead. I'll send an advance party after you, to stop everyone traveling the road either way. I don't want anybody, soldier or civilian, running to the Federals with a whisper about us."

Still mystified, Shadburne carried out orders. By noon they came to the muddy tree-cloaked banks of the Blackwater, broad and turbid at that point. The old stone piers of the wrecked bridge rose in mid-current, but the timbers and flooring had been ripped away and scattered along the banks.

"Excellent," approved Hampton, riding in among the Iron Scouts. "Since they pulled the bridge down, they thought they needn't put a guard here. Where's my engineering officer? Send someone to bring Lieutenant Lannau up, and his special crew with him."

Lieutenant Lannau reported. He commanded forty riders, who bore axes, crowbars, and coils of rope at their saddles. Under Lannau's direction they began to drag together the dismantled timbers and cut new ones. As they labored, the main body closed up along the road, and was allowed to dismount and rest the horses. But complete silence was sternly commanded.

"Quiet, everybody," Clay heard an officer warning.

"Put away that mouth organ, Private House. Yes, you men can eat, but no fires. What have you got there, Lefler? Sweet potatoes? You'll have to gobble them down raw; we daren't show a smoke."

It was dark when Lannau saluted Hampton and pronounced the bridge ready.

"Then we move out," announced Hampton. "Shadburne, how far are we from Coggin's Point?"

"About ten miles, sir."

"We'll advance slowly, but we'll be all right. With Grant gone, the guard won't be so vigilant. I want to charge in after midnight, when everybody's at his sleepiest."

They started across the bridge. It trembled, but stood up under the horses.

"Which way to that cavalry camp between the cattle and City Point?" Hampton was asking.

"The center road, sir," Shadburne told him. "They're at Sycamore Church."

"General Rosser, head along there and hit them. Take two guns with you. Rooney Lee, the other two guns go with you—take the first turn left, cut up any opposition you find, and be ready to defend us when we come back with the cattle. The rest of the column heads right, and when we hear General Rosser attack that cavalry camp we'll go in for our beef."

It happened exactly that way. Clay was with the advance force that stole unchallenged to the very edge of the sprawling row of pens beside the James. Midnight was past, and the squadrons waited for what seemed an eternity in the dark when, off to the left, sudden flashes trembled in the black sky and the guns roared.

"Come on!" whooped Shadburne, and spurred his horse to a gallop.

Clay sent Cherokee after his sergeant, and the two of them were the first to reach a rail-fenced pen. They jumped down and began to drag the rails to the ground. Somewhere a frightened voice yelled. An unarmed cattle tender held up his hands as Prioleau shoved a pistol under his very nose.

The racket of guns at the cavalry camp seemed to shake the earth, but Clay and Shadburne were inside the pen, slapping the plump flanks of drowsy cattle.

"Hi! Hi!" Clay yelled at the top of his voice. "Get moving, you steers!"

The nearest of the animals moved stumblingly through the breached rails. Others, wakening, followed them instinctively. Clay ran ahead of them and mounted Cherokee. Shadburne yelled, his voice a high quavering howl.

"Yippeeee! Hooray for Texas! I never thought I'd be punching cattle this far from home!"

"Head them toward Sycamore Church!" an officer was thundering. "The fight's already over down there!"

The road seemed full of cattle as Clay rode along its edge. He tore a branch from a tree and used it to keep the steers in line. Around him was confusion, but it was exultant confusion. Elsewhere in the retreating mass came captured wagons. Hugh Scott rode alongside one, bent toward it, and shoved his arm inside the cover.

"This is a sutler's wagon!" he cried. "I'll bet its owner wishes he'd obeyed Grant's orders to stay home. Here, Clay, get your saddlebag open. You can have these boxes of sardines, and here's something that looks like a bottle of syrup. Stow 'em away. Now, take this smoked tongue, and maybe this is candy—"

An officer spurred at them, yelling for them to get away from the wagon, but not before they had filled their pockets and saddlebags with delicacies.

In the dawn, Hampton's men found themselves back at the rebuilt bridge. The Federals had recovered and were trying to pursue, but Rooney Lee's force, between the stolen herd and the enemy, had checked that pursuit. The whole road thronged for miles with cattle, big bulky creatures over which gray troopers licked their bearded lips. As they approached their own lines, Calbraith Butler, with the regiments left in camp, rode out to help herd the treasure in.

There was hearty celebration of the feat, though men, horses, and steers alike were weary from that flight away from Coggin's Point. The cattle were allowed to graze in a great meadow near the railroad, with squads of riders strung around the edge of the vast herd. A plump commissary officer arrived from Robert E. Lee's headquarters. He saluted Wade Hampton with undisguised awe.

"General, this is a victory worth Cold Harbor or Reams Station," said the commissary. "It's all right to tell you a secret now—when you started after this herd, the Army of Northern Virginia had only fifteen days' rations of meat, and short rations at that. My men have counted the steers, and we make it exactly two thousand, eight hundred, and forty-six."

"You'd better cut that down to two thousand, eight hundred, and forty-five," remarked Calbraith Butler. "Sergeant Shadburne and his Iron Scouts have just butchered a big fat one."

The commissary goggled fiercely. "That's against regulations!" he spluttered. "Who's that sergeant? General Hampton, you'll surely court-martial him."

"Not Shadburne," said Hampton, with one of his rare laughs. "He found the cattle and led us to them. His men deserve the best."

Just then he saw Clay passing close at hand.

"Buckner!" he called, and Clay approached and stood at attention.

"Shadburne says that this was your idea," General Hampton told him.

"Not exactly, sir," said Clay. "We were just talking about rations that would walk of themselves, and that suggested the cattle herd at Coggin's Point."

Hampton scribbled rapidly on a leaf of his order book, tore the paper out, and held it toward Clay.

"That's a ten-day furlough for you," he said.

Thankfully Clay took the paper and went looking for his friends. They were cutting up the carcass of the steer, which hung from the big branch of a tree. Shadburne grinned congratulations at news of the furlough.

"You'll be seeing the Winsteads in Richmond, I suppose?"

"That's right," Clay said. "I'll take them some little knicknacks from that sutler wagon."

"Pick some flowers to give Miss Lark," teased Hugh Scott.

"Wait, here's a more welcome bouquet than that," declared Hennegan.

He held out a noble rib roast.

"Wrap that up to give your hostess, Clay. And maybe a couple of sirloin steaks, and some shins to boil. Help me fix him up a real present, boys."

Knives in hand, the Iron Scouts carved and wrapped up a dozen choice morsels.

"You'll be the most popular guest in any Richmond home," predicted Shadburne. "Have a good time, Clay, and remember us to the Winsteads."

❧ 12 ❧
Enemy Railroads

Clay's friends in Richmond greeted him happily. When he produced his great cargo of beef, Mrs. Winstead decreed that the greater part of it must go to the army hospitals.

"It will make whole kettles of broth, just what those poor hungry soldiers should have to get back their strength," she said.

"The steaks won't make much broth," pleaded Clay. "Remember, I'm a poor hungry soldier, too. I think we ought to have those steaks for our own dinner tonight."

Lark sat next to him at the table, answering his questions. "Mrs. Parmenter has been banished through the lines," she informed him. "It was decided not to keep her prisoner. Maybe mercy shown to a Yankee spy will be repaid by mercy, on the other side, toward some captured Southerner."

"What happened to Towers?" Clay asked.

"Nobody has heard of him since his arrest," replied Lark. "That may mean that he won't be executed. But we know about Rowena Croft. She's engaged to be married."

"Good for her," applauded Clay. "Probably she captured some handsome, glittering young staff officer."

"No such capture," said Dr. Winstead from the head of the table. "She's going to marry a simple corporal of infantry in a hard-fighting Georgia regiment. Everybody's surprised, but she and her corporal are happy."

When dessert came in, Dr. Winstead addressed Clay again.

"I've been exchanging letters with your father and mother," he said. "They've invited me to send Mrs. Winstead and Celie and Lark down to your home in North Carolina, and we've decided to accept."

"That's splendid!" cried Clay. "I know my folks want to repay all the things you all have done for me. And it's safe and peaceful down yonder in Northampton County."

"Your people insist that it will be no imposition," amplified the doctor. "They say that crops have been good and nobody's in actual want."

"That's hard for you to realize up here in Richmond," ventured Clay.

"Yes," agreed Dr. Winstead, "rations get shorter every day since Grant put us under siege and occupied the farms around the town. I'll stay up here on my hospital duty, but I'll feel happier with my folks all those long miles away from the fighting."

On the last day of Clay's furlough, he and Dr. Winstead saw the three ladies off at the depot. At the very doorstep of the car, Lark put her slim hand in Clay's broad one.

"I won't tell you to be careful," she said. "The Iron Scouts aren't noted for being careful. But try to be lucky."

"You'll enjoy yourself at my home, I know," Clay told her. "Kiss my mother for me."

"I will," Lark promised. "Now I'll kiss you for her."

She put her hands on his shoulders, and her lips brushed his cheek.

"And this is just for us," she whispered softly.

Another light touch on his other cheek, and she was gone. The train chugged away southward. Clay and Dr. Winstead watched it out of sight.

"That leaves just us men to fight the war," observed the old doctor, stumping away. "But has it occurred to you, my boy, that the women are about as good at this war as the men?"

"Some of them are better," agreed Clay.

The next day he bade good-by to Dr. Winstead and returned to Blackwater Swamp. For two months he helped to scout toward Federal headquarters.

Shadburne worked his subordinates hard, and they uncovered much information valuable to Lee and Hampton. As winter closed in, the cavalrymen built log huts at their positions along the railroad. In Blackwater Swamp the squashy mud of the summer had begun to freeze by late November, when Shadburne drew Clay aside for a conference.

"Things are slow here," said Shadburne. "There isn't

a lot of raiding and marching and counter-marching. Headquarters wants a full report on the condition of the enemy's railroad system up above Richmond. I've been told to pick a man to go behind their lines with me, and I want you."

"Me?" cried Clay. "But there are a dozen Iron Scouts who have spent more time in Northern Virginia than I have."

"That's one important reason I want you. Lots of us are fairly well known to the Federals. I'm going to mow my whiskers down to disguise myself as a civilian, and I can count on your being a stranger to most of the men on the other side. We'll wear shabby clothes and pretend to be refugees from the cruel Confederates. Are you game?"

Shadburne left Dick Hogan to command in Blackwater Swamp. Jim Sloan had bought Shadburne's best horse, paying for it with a promissory note for two hundred dollars from the next treasure of Federal greenbacks captured, and Clay asked Sloan to look after Cherokee, too. Shadburne trimmed his long shabby beard to a genteel point, which made him look milder and younger. They put on nondescript suits and hats and overcoats, traveled up through Petersburg and beyond Richmond. One morning in the first week in December, they slipped away through the line of defending infantry above the capital. By Shadburne's special requests, yells and shots rang out behind them as they fled through brush and high weeds, tumbled down a bank, and found themselves looking into the muzzle of a musket.

"Stand still, both of you!" warned the blue infantry-man who held the musket, and called for his corporal, who marched the two back to a fire where a picket reserve gathered.

"Who are you?" demanded the corporal. "Where are your papers?"

"We don't have any papers," replied Shadburne. "We're lucky to have just ourselves. The Confederates had warrants out for our arrest in Richmond, and we barely escaped."

From the picket post they were taken to headquarters at a farmhouse to be questioned by a captain, then by a colonel. Shadburne did most of the talking, and did it extremely well.

"My brother and I always swore we'd never fight against the Union," he explained plausibly. "I was able to convince them I was sick, but my young brother here just came of draft age. I helped him sneak away from the conscription officers, and we sneaked out of town. We didn't know there were Union troops here."

"What Confederate forces are holding Richmond?" the colonel asked.

"Why, sir, I can't rightly say," replied Shadburne, the very spirit of candor. He turned to Clay. "Hosea, how many soldiers do you think there are in Richmond?"

"I don't know how to answer that," confessed Clay, crinkling his brow. "I've been hiding from the soldiers, not counting them."

"Fifty thousand?" prompted the colonel. "Sixty thousand?"

"Well," said Shadburne, "fifty or sixty thousand, yes, sir. Or more or less."

"These men might be spies," growled the captain. "Do you two realize that you might get court-martialed and shot?"

"We could have got that done to us in Richmond without coming here," replied Clay.

"They're more likely just honest fools," said the colonel, shaking his handsome head. "Otherwise they'd have some kind of forged identification. How does it happen that neither of you has so much as a scrap of writing on you?"

"Paper's right scarce in Richmond, sir," replied Shadburne, "and ink is scarcer."

"There's plenty of paper in Richmond," argued the captain. He fixed Clay with a suspicious eye. "Don't you know that our soldiers trade newspapers with the rebels all the time?"

"Why," said Clay respectfully, "I can't either read or write, so I don't look at any newspapers."

Both the officers chuckled at that. Then the colonel asked: "Since you got away from the rebels, what do you propose to do?"

"I'm a horse doctor," Shadburne informed him. "I figured I might get something to do in that line with the Union cavalry, and my brother could help me. Show him how to do a thing and he'll do it."

"Veterinarian, eh? We might use you, at that. We'll see."

Clay and Shadburne remained at the house the rest of the day, ate at the officers' mess, and were questioned by the colonel perhaps a dozen times. About noon of the following day the colonel summoned them to his office and handed each a written sheet of paper.

"This headquarters is transferring to Fredericksburg, and there's a couple of transportation vouchers to allow you to come along. We'll let the provost up there talk to you, and if he says you're all right maybe you can do some horse doctoring at the calvary remount base." He raised his voice. "Sergeant Brubach!"

A stocky noncommissioned officer with an enormous roan-gray mustache came in and saluted.

"These two civilians are in your charge," the colonel said. "You'll see them into the provost marshal's hands at Fredericksburg." To Shadburne he added: "Convince the provost of your sincerity, and he'll help you get assigned to the veterinary service."

The two trudged away in the wake of Sergeant Brubach. As the sergeant's broad form rounded the corner of the house ahead of them, Shadburne touched Clay on the elbow and plunged into a clump of holly bushes. Clay followed him for four thorn-pricking leaps, then the two found themselves trotting through pine woods.

"The railroad passes within half a mile of here," whispered Shadburne. "We'll catch a train, but not one that goes to Fredericksburg and not under the eye of any sergeant named Brubach."

They came to where the railroad moved northwestward through a cut in the tree-grown landscape. A rickety shed stood there, and on a bench inside lay several signal flags rolled together. As they examined these, a steam whistle sounded around a bend to eastward.

"Here comes transportation, and we have vouchers," said Shadburne, and stepped out beside the tracks, waving a red-patterned flag. A locomotive puffed into sight, trailing a string of boxcars. As Shadburne waved, the locomotive screeched to a halt, and down jumped the engineer. Black and greasy and truculent, he rushed toward them.

"Why did you flag us down?" he blustered. "We're supposed to switch west at Hanover Junction with this train of supplies. We don't stop for anybody this side of the Blue Ridge."

"We know all about that," Shadburne told him bleakly. "We're to go with you and investigate. Here's our authority."

He shoved the paper the colonel had given him under the engineer's sooty nose. "See the signature? We'll ride in the cab with you. You're to answer a few questions."

"Oh," grumbled the engineer, "you're one of them inspectors. All right, come along."

They rode with the engineer all afternoon and into the night. Shadburne belabored engineer and fireman with questions, and he and Clay learned a great deal about the Federal army's transport system—rebuilt roads from Alexandria and Manassas to Front Royal, Fredericksburg, and Culpeper, with swarms of locomotives and miles of cars to bring supplies to the far-flung blue legions. At Gordonsville Shadburne and Clay stepped down from the locomotive cab in the gloom. On another siding a train panted as men crowded aboard.

"Come on," said Shadburne, and they, too, climbed into a car jammed with soldiers, knapsacks, and muskets. An officer glanced carelessly at their transportation vouchers and left them alone. They crossed the Rapidan above Orange Court House, trundled through Culpeper and Brandy Station, and at midnight passed the Rappahannock. At a small depot on the far side Shadburne and Clay left the train. It was dark and cold, and a shivery wind tried to creep under their tight-buttoned overcoats.

"We're no more than a couple of hours' walk from Captain Crofut's," said Shadburne. "Suppose we go sleep in his barn and ask him for breakfast tomorrow morning."

The chill of the night quickened their march. Unchallenged, they found the farm and thankfully snuggled into a mowful of hay. When Crofut appeared to feed his stock at dawn, they startled him with greetings, and soon they were happily devouring ham, eggs, and coffee in the kitchen.

"From here it's maybe twenty-five miles to the camps above Fredericksburg," computed Shadburne. "Suppose we leave at sundown, travel all night, and lay up the next day before going on. I want to ride back toward Richmond on whatever kind of railroad the Federals are running. Now, Captain Crofut, what favor can we do you?"

"A big one, if you will," was the reply. "If you think it's too dangerous, I'll understand. Carry some letters for us."

"Letters?" repeated Clay.

Crofut pulled a drawer out of a desk and, from a recess behind, drew a small sheaf of papers, folded and sealed and addressed.

"These are from families in the neighborhood to their friends and kinsmen in the Confederate army," he said. "I gathered them up, hoping for a way to smuggle them back."

"They'll get to Richmond if we do," promised Shadburne. "Divide them into two packages, and Clay and I will each take one. Then, if something happens to one of us, the other will bring part of the letters through with him."

The letters were divided into two equal sheafs, wrapped and fastened with sealing wax. That evening at sundown Clay and Shadburne shook hands with their host and accepted a generous package of bread and meat. Then they struck off down the Rappahannock.

It was by no means as difficult and furtive a journey as they had known in past years, when that part of Virginia was fought over by the opposing armies and every crossroads was haunted by cavalry pickets. They arrived at dawn at an old Iron Scout camp of 1863 and found a hut still in good repair. Lighting a fire on the hearth, they drowsed away the day, ate the last of their provisions for supper, and left at dusk. Again they stole forward in the night, hour after hour. It was perhaps ten o'clock when they paused and looked at great circles and clumps of firelight against the dark sky to eastward.

"That's where the Yankees have their big base camps across the river from Fredericksburg," said Shadburne. "No reason to go in there if we can avoid it. Let's see if we can find a boat along the shore, then get into town, locate the depot, and ride as close to Richmond as we can."

At the foot of a path at the river's brink a skiff was tied up. They cut it loose and drifted downstream with it. On one side they could see the massed radiance of the campfires, on the other the paler lights of Fredericksburg. Shadburne, paddling with an oar, headed them toward the south bank.

"That looks like a wharf up ahead," he said to Clay. Grab hold when we touch and let's get on shore again. If anybody asks a question, we're just two harmless civilians with transportation vouchers. Show your paper and they'll let you pass."

Clay caught the edge of the wharf, vaulted up, and gave Shadburne a hand to help him out of the boat. They walked across the planks and up the slope beyond.

"Halt!" a sentry challenged them. "Who goes there?"

"Friends," replied Clay. "Civilians."

"Where did you come from?"

"We rowed across from the north shore. We're headed for the railroad station."

"Sergeant, do you want to talk to these men?"

Several other soldiers ambled close in the darkness, and beyond them approached a stocky man holding a lantern. Clay saw stripes on the blue sleeve, and the light revealed a broad face and luxuriant mustaches.

It was Sergeant Brubach.

ᕗ 13 ᕗ

Caught and Recognized

The sergeant came close to Shadburne and Clay, holding the lantern high.

"Who are you?" he demanded. "What are you doing on the river?"

"Just trying to get off it, Major," said Shadburne plausibly.

"Don't you know that nobody crosses it without a permit?" Brubach persisted. "Civilians in particular. Wait a minute—I remember you two horse doctors."

"Horse doctors?" repeated Shadburne, with a fine show of mystification. "We don't know what you mean."

"Yes, you do. You were supposed to come along with the headquarters detail, but you sneaked away. Better come along to the colonel."

"How far is it?" asked Shadburne, his voice suddenly faint. "I've been sick, weak—can't walk."

He sounded so wretched that Clay felt a new apprehension, but Sergeant Brubach only said, "You were paddling mighty strong out yonder on the Rappahannock."

"Let me have a drink from the river and maybe I'll feel better," pleaded Shadburne, facing back the way they had come.

"Here's my canteen," said one of the soldiers, offering it. Shadburne put out a shaky hand for it, then suddenly collapsed, just at the edge of the wharf. He seemed on the point of rolling down the bank.

All attention turned toward his fallen body. Clay tightened his sinews for a jump into the darkness, but he could not desert Shadburne, suddenly so ill. He flung down his bundle of letters and with a quick movement of his toe slid it under the boards of the wharf. A couple of soldiers gently lifted Shadburne, and one held a canteen to his lips.

"Thanks, thanks," Shadburne was half-whispering. "I feel better now."

"Help your friend," Sergeant Brubach ordered Clay, and Clay supported Shadburne with an arm around his waist. A soldier held Shadburne's other elbow, and the party headed into the town.

"Are you all right?" Clay asked his friend anxiously.

"Since I flung those letters into the river, yes," Shadburne whispered almost inaudibly.

"I got rid of mine, too," Clay whispered back.

"Never mind telling each other secrets," called out Brubach gruffly. "Come on, here's our office."

A door opened and lamplight streamed out. Brubach talked to a sentry, then beckoned Shadburne and Clay inside.

From an inner room emerged the colonel who had

given them transportation vouchers several days earlier. He looked at Shadburne, then at Clay.

"Yes, Sergeant Brubach, I seem to remember these men. Bring them here into the light. Why did you run off from us when we were going to bring you here? What's your name, you with the pointed beard?"

"James Taylor, sir," replied Shadburne.

"That's a false name, I'll wager. Search these two prisoners."

Hands dived into Clay's pockets, under his coat, into his collar. The search yielded a roll of greenbacks, the transportation voucher, one or two other trifles. Clay stood still, marveling at his own sense of calm. Suddenly Sergeant Brubach, who had been searching Shadburne, exclaimed triumphantly and offered the colonel a folded paper.

"It was stuck inside the cuff of his overcoat, sir."

The colonel spread it out on his table. "A promissory note," he told the others. "Signed by somebody named James Sloan, acknowledging a debt of two hundred dollars to—what's this—"

He glanced up in sudden triumph.

"To George D. Shadburne!" he almost yelled. "So you're really Shadburne of the Iron Scouts!"

"Get another couple of men in here," snapped Brubach to the sentry at the door, and two soldiers entered, muskets at the ready.

"Shadburne," the colonel said again. "I know that name. I've heard it again and again this fall—they say you planned that cattle-stealing raid in September. Well, we have you at last. Splendid!"

"Do you think you have Shadburne?" was the cool rejoinder. "You've just got a note that says somebody owes him money. I bought it from Shadburne a month ago, at a discount of twenty per cent. But—"

"That won't do," the colonel broke him off. "You're identified. Who's your friend here? Probably he's overdue on the gallows, just like you."

"My name is Taylor," repeated Shadburne stubbornly. "I'm a civilian and a noncombatant and a refugee from inside the rebel lines. If you think I'm guilty of anything that Shadburne has done, put me on trial. I'll fetch a dozen reputable citizens who know my real name."

"And who are you?" the colonel asked Clay. "Wait a second, don't bother to give me a false name. It so happens that there's somebody who knows the Iron Scouts by sight."

He dipped pen in ink and wrote swiftly.

"Sergeant," he said to Brubach, "there's a supply steamer heading downriver to Fort Monroe and around the Peninsula to general headquarters at City Point. I'm relieving you of duty here, to see these men go on that steamer, under guard, to General Grant's provost marshal. This note is for him."

He handed the paper to Brubach, who saluted, his mustache bristling with energy, then beckoned Clay and Shadburne to the door.

"We're going on a little journey," announced Brubach, "and this time there'll be no absent-minded wandering away on your part. Four of us will guard you with loaded guns and fixed bayonets. Don't try to run, unless you want to carry along some steel and lead."

"We aren't Iron Scouts," said Shadburne again.

"Maybe not. But if you are, we'll find out. Meanwhile, you don't leave me beyond arm's length until I turn you over to the man who's waiting for you."

They traveled all that night and all the next day on the splintered deck of a shabby little steamer, among heaped bales and crates of military supplies. Their guards lounged close around them, muskets in hand. Never were fewer than two of the detail present and awake until the boat tied up at the wharf at Fort Monroe, down at the tip of the Virginia Peninsula. Then Sergeant Brubach and two of the men departed for a few moments, leaving but one soldier with Clay and Shadburne.

"It's kind of cold, huh?" inquired the guard, squinting up at a dull gray sky. "If I feel the chill, coming from up in Connecticut, you two Southerners ought to be shivering."

"We'd shiver if we didn't think you'd call us scared," replied Clay.

"Look, take this blanket." The Connecticut man unfastened it from his knapsack and tossed it to them. "Wrap it around your legs, the two of you."

"We don't want to deprive you, friend," said Shadburne.

"Go on, take it. I'm warmer than you are—these winter uniforms are wool and an inch thick."

Shadburne pulled the blanket over his lap and Clay's. "You've got real heart in you, Yank," he said thankfully.

A friendly laugh in the dimness. "Shucks, they issue us hearts in the Union army just the way they do with the Confeds. Why should I make you suffer any more than you've got to be suffering? I feel sorry for any prisoner of war."

"You do?" said Clay, half-uncomprehendingly, and their guard laughed again.

"Nothing would make me feel any better than to see you two gone safe home, and me safe home, too. I'm a poor man, but I'd feel rich if I could see my own place in Connecticut again."

"You're poor?" repeated Shadburne. "What would you think of a hundred dollars in greenbacks?"

"I'd think it was eight months' pay for a private in the infantry. Not that I ever saw a hundred dollars in one chunk."

"How would you like to see it?" asked Shadburne, leaning forward. "Give me a piece of paper and I'll write you a note to a friend of mine in Washington. He'll put the hundred right in your hand."

"Just like that?" inquired the guard. "For nothing?"

"We-ell," said Shadburne slowly, "you'd

deserve some kind of pay for turning your back and letting one of us hit you—very softly, behind the ear. And you'd have to lie quiet and stunned till you were dead certain we'd jumped over the side and had swum at least a hundred yards away."

"A hundred greenback dollars," said the soldier again.

With his left hand he fumbled a bit of paper and a stubby pencil from his blouse pocket.

"Write that message to your friend," he said.

Shadburne did so, and tossed it back to the friendly guard. Just then Sergeant Brubach returned with the other two.

"These men tried to bribe me, Sarge," reported the guard at once. "Here's the name of a friend of theirs who was to give me my pay."

Shadburne groaned aloud, and Sergeant Brubach chuckled.

"All right," he said, "they've cleared enough truck out of the hold so that you two can ride there the rest of the way. Come on down, now you've learned that we can't be bought."

In the hold, Clay and Shadburne stretched out unhappily on the borrowed blankets. The guard from Connecticut fetched them some bread and fried bacon.

"Don't hold this business against me," he pleaded, as though to old friends. "I was bound to tell how you wanted to escape. Wouldn't you have done the same in my place?"

"I'll have to admit that I would," agreed Clay.

"Then make your friend stop scowling. He scares me."

"I'm not scowling at you," Shadburne told him. "I'm just mad at myself for writing down the name of my friend in Washington. Now he'll be arrested."

"Yes, I'm afraid he will," nodded the soldier. "I sure do hate all this locking up of people. I feel like I don't have nothing but the key to associate with."

That night, too, they steamed through the darkness. Shadburne and Clay slept. They woke at the nudgings of the friendly guard, and mounted to the deck.

It was bright day, and they had come to City Point. They looked at a whole river full of masted ships at anchor, a wharf at which their little steamer was moored, and beyond the wharf a rise of ground crowded with sheds and tents. A Union flag fluttered above the largest building. Blue uniforms moved everywhere, on wharfs, ships, and land.

"Yonder's the headquarters of General Grant," announced Brubach. "Come on, you prisoners. Men, watch every move they make."

They tramped down a gangplank to the wharf, and in silence mounted to a hard-beaten path that led westward to the tongue of land that gave City Point its name. Were they heading for Grant's headquarters? Clay decided not to ask, not to speak any word. Nearly at the large building, in front of a small structure of rough boards, Brubach gestured for them to halt.

"Provost's office," he said. "Go on in."

They obeyed. A trig-uniformed military clerk accepted the folded message Brubach offered, and went through a door to an office beyond. A moment later he returned, and after him hurried a middle-sized man whose blue tunic bore the insignia of a lieutenant colonel.

"Hello there, Shadburne," he called out in a voice of happy greeting. "And my old friend, Clay Buckner."

He offered a welcoming hand. Clay stared at a pleasant, wise face, framed in neat brown side whiskers, and he knew that face.

"You're Tryon, the spy!" he gasped out.

"Tryon, the head of Sheridan's scouts," Shadburne cried.

"I was both of those things, but not any more," said Tryon merrily. "You Iron Scouts drove me out of the spy business, and the scout business, too. I'm Lieutenant Colonel Tryon now, provost at City Point."

He glanced at the paper in his hand.

"They wanted me to identify you positively as Iron Scouts. Come on into my office, gentlemen, and sit down. We have so much gossip to trade."

≫ 14 ≪
The Prison Barge

Brubach stood and stared uncomprehendingly. Even his mustache sagged with mystification.

"It's all right, Sergeant Brubach. These are old friendly enemies of mine." Colonel Tryon was laughing. "I don't know any two rebels I'd rather entertain here at my headquarters. But suppose somebody just handcuffs them together, to be sure they don't ungratefully slip away before we get tired of their company."

From a desk drawer the clerk produced a pair of heavy iron bracelets, joined by a stout chain some eighteen inches long. He clamped one bracelet around Clay's right wrist, the other around Shadburne's left wrist. He turned a key in each lock in turn, then slid the key into his hip pocket.

"Are they really Iron Scouts, Colonel Tryon?" Brubach asked. "If they are, I've heard orders that say they're to be hanged at once."

But Tryon laughed again, and shook his head.

"Those orders are out of date," he said. "I remember how, about sixteen months ago, we were going to hang young Buckner here. But it so happened that I myself was in Shadburne's hands, and Shadburne was ready to hang me if Buckner swung off. So they traded us against each other. No, Sergeant Brubach, no gallows for these gentlemen. I don't want to start a series of hangings on both sides."

He motioned toward the inner door. "Come on in, I say." He beckoned to the clerk. "Stand behind them, with a pistol in your hand. You men who brought them, better stay within earshot, and keep your weapons ready. Iron Scouts are champion at escaping."

Inside Tryon's office was a desk. Sliding behind it, Tryon picked up a tin coffeepot.

"Join me," he invited, and filled tin mugs. Then he sat down. Clay and Shadburne took their cups in their unchained hands. Still Tryon grinned, the picture of a happy host.

"Some of my men recognized you and your friends during that beef raid," he told Shadburne. "I don't suppose you can give us back our cattle?"

"I can guarantee you won't get them back," replied Shadburne. "They were cut up into steaks and roasts long ago, and the Army of Northern Virginia ate them up."

"All except for a few chunks I took to Richmond with me for the Winsteads," put in Clay.

"And how are the Winsteads?" inquired Tryon. "How is that brave young girl, Miss Lark?"

"She's certain that our side will win the war," Clay told him.

Tryon picked up something from a tray on his desk. "Remember this, Clay Buckner?"

"It's your penknife," said Clay at once.

"Your penknife, really. I remember making you a present of it."

"They took it away from me when I was captured last year," said Clay.

"I know. I got it back, for a souvenir." Tryon tossed the knife down again. "All right, gentlemen, I promise you that nobody will hang you so long as I'm provost here. What will you do for me in return?"

"We'll say 'thank you,'" Shadburne answered.

"No more than that? But the war's over so far as you're concerned. Why not be as friendly as I've been, and tell us something about the dispositions of your troops around Petersburg?"

"We don't agree that the war's over for us, Colonel Tryon," said Shadburne, leaning forward to set down his empty coffee mug. "Sorry, but we'll not give you any military information."

"Too bad." Tryon addressed the clerk. "These men will have to be locked up. General Grant's inspecting the troops, and I think he may want to question them when he gets back tomorrow. Put them on the *Walkil*."

"Down in the hold with the other prisoners, sir?" asked the clerk.

"No, no," and Tryon shook his head. "There are a dozen rebels already in that hold, and this pair of sportsmen probably would organize them to break out. Put them in that cabin that used to be the office. The porthole's barred, isn't it? See that they have blankets and food, but no fire in the stove. If it gets cold in there, give them more blankets; but, I repeat, no fire. I wouldn't put it past them to try to burn their way out."

"And the shackles—" the clerk began.

"Sorry, but those shackles had better stay on." Tryon rose. "Gentlemen, I must bid you good-bye for the time being. Probably I'll be taking you to General Grant some time tomorrow."

"Come on, prisoners," said the clerk.

Brubach and the three privates who had guarded them all the way from Fredericksburg accompanied them as they walked back to the wharf. Suddenly Shadburne nudged Clay.

"Look yonder," he said, and Clay saw a great flat hulk at the water's edge, from which huge laden wagons were being rolled ashore.

"That's a pontoon train," said Shadburne. "Somebody reckons on crossing rivers somewhere. Which way are those pontoons headed?"

"Where you won't follow them," Brubach assured them. "Come aboard here."

They were marched up a plank to the deck of a large barge, and were met by a sentry with his musket at the shoulder. Tryon's clerk spoke to an officer, then opened the heavy door of a cabin.

"In you get," he said, gesturing Shadburne and Clay inside. "Colonel Tryon said no fire in the stove, but you might be comfortable if you stand near that inner bulkhead. The galley's on the other side of it, and it's always boiling hot in there."

The cabin was not much more than a cell, about eight feet by ten. A pair of cots and an old desk took up most of the room. A single square porthole, with a glass pane on a hinge to swing inward, looked westward toward Grant's headquarters. Two steel bars rose from sill to sill in front of it. Soldiers fetched in blankets to throw on the cots.

"You're under watch every moment," the clerk warned them as he paused on the doorsill. "If you make any noise even, you'll be in big trouble."

"How can we be in any bigger trouble than we are right now?" Clay inquired.

"Better not try to find out."

The clerk was gone. He closed the door behind him, and they heard the big lock grate as it fastened them in.

"Look, Clay," mumbled Shadburne softly, and held out his free right hand. In its palm lay the penknife Tryon had showed them.

"Where did you get that?"

"Keep your voice down. I snapped it up when I put my coffee mug on his desk. Let me see what I can do about these iron bracelets."

But their shackles were of heavy steel, and the knife point barely scratched them. Clay glanced toward the port, then put out his left hand to take up something from the desk.

"A penholder," he announced. "A silver penholder."

I remember that Tryon said this used to be an office."

Shadburne took the holder, studied it carefully, and tested its texture with the knife.

"It's soft," he reported. "It can be whittled. Maybe we're not so safely shut up as they think. Didn't both these bracelets lock with the same key?"

"Yes," said Clay. "I saw that clerk put the key in his pocket, though."

"Well, maybe I can butcher a key out of this holder as soon as it gets dark. Swing that sash shut, the breeze is right cold."

Clay shut the sash and fastened its latch. Together they gazed out through the glass. More soldiers were disembarking at a nearby wharf, their big transport looming above the prison barge.

"Look at all the equipment they're carrying," pointed out Clay. "Heavy knapsacks and overcoats, and two cartridge boxes each."

"They're getting ready to make a march somewhere," judged Shadburne. "Troops aren't put into that kind of marching order to go into their forts around Petersburg. That looks more like a long-distance raid somewhere. But whereabouts?"

"What difference does it make whereabouts?" asked Clay wretchedly. "We can't carry word to anyone."

"Don't be too sure."

The December night was falling. Drops of rain struck the deck. Outside the barred port, a soldier walked along the deck of the barge, lighting lanterns and hanging them to the rail. When he had gone, Shadburne pulled open the sash and carefully studied the bars of the port.

"Close together, but maybe not too close," he pronounced. "If a man wriggled through on edge now—"

"We're chained together," objected Clay.

"I know that. But maybe not for long."

Sitting on the edge of one of the cots where the lantern light would strike from outside, Shadburne began to whittle at the silver penholder with the knife he had purloined. Long bright shreds and slivers of metal came away. Scraping the end of the holder flat, Shadburne prodded it at the keyhole on the shackle, then whittled again and tried to fit it as before.

"Here comes somebody," warned Clay, and Shadburne quickly shoved penholder and knife under the blankets on the cot.

A soldier unlocked the door and pushed it open, then stood there with his bayonet ready. Another man entered, a pudgy man in an apron with his sleeves rolled up, laden with food. He carried a plate in one hand, and balanced another plate on his wrist and forearm. In his other hand he carried two mugs of coffee, and they smelled good.

"Sorry we can't give you knives and forks," he said. "but the officer of the day told us you'd probably carve away the bulkhead and escape. So spoons is what you eat with."

Clay accepted one heaping plate. "It looks tasty," he commented.

"Better rations than you rebels generally get, huh?"

said the pudgy man, setting the coffee mugs on the desk. "Fried salt pork and toasted hardtack and beans. We're tired of it in our army."

"Because you've got lots of it," suggested Shadburne, taking a spoonful of beans.

"Tons," the man laughed. "Why, the whole Fifth Corps is cooking up six days' rations of pork this minute."

He was gone, and the door locked behind him. Shadburne took another bite. Clay saw his eyes gleam in the light from the lantern outside.

"Six days' rations being cooked out there, he said," Shadburne growled. "That fits in with the pontoons we saw."

"It means a march, all right," agreed Clay.

"The whole Fifth Corps," repeated Shadburne. "Twenty-five thousand Federal soldiers. Clay, we've got to get out of here."

He swigged his coffee hastily, then returned to scraping and hacking at the silver penholder. Clay ate and drank more slowly, watching the port. Wearily it rained out there. A sentry passed, his chin drawn down into the collar of his overcoat.

"Start counting slowly," said Shadburne, as the sentry cleared the port.

Clay did not ask why, but began to say numbers under his breath. Shadburne paused in his work to grab mouthfuls of meat and beans, then gouged at the penholder again. The sentry came back into view and tramped outside the port.

"How far did you count?" Shadburne asked.

"Three hundred and sixteen," Clay told him.

"Call it three hundred and twenty. Start again."

Clay did so, while Shadburne continued his labors. When the sentry's shadow came around again, he had counted three hundred and eighteen.

"We can figure on about how often he crosses in front of our porthole," said Shadburne. "How fast were you counting?"

"About as fast as the drillmaster counts for you to march."

"Two counts to a second, then. About two and a half minutes to a tour around the deck for that sentry. Maybe there's one minute, or near to it, when he isn't in sight."

"But others will be in sight," suggested Clay.

"Wait until it's really late at night, and dark and cold, with all this rain. Then there'll be nobody stirring out except that sentry on duty."

Shadburne had scraped and rubbed for a painstaking hour, and at last he had reduced the tip of the silver holder to a thin narrow strip of metal. He tried it once again, and crooned with satisfaction when he saw that it went into the keyhole of the steel shackle on his wrist.

"I wish we had some black lead or something, to show where the lands of the lock—the ridges and spaces— come inside," he said.

"There's soot on the bottom of this coffee mug," Clay told him.

Shadburne took the mug and smeared soot heavily on both sides of the silver strip, then dragged Clay with

him to the very sill of the porthole and experimented
by putting the strip into the keyhole and cautiously ap-
plying pressure in one direction, then the other. When
he brought the strip out again, a pattern of bright lines
showed in the soot.

"That shows where the lands of the lock come," said
Shadburne happily.

More scraping and gouging, with greater care than
before. Again and again Shadburne experimented with
the key he was fashioning. At first it refused to turn in
the lock, but he continued to saw at the notches he had
made. Finally he grinned happily over the manacles.

"I think we've got it," he said. "Give me a scrap of
that fat pork."

From a leftover rind on one of the plates he squeezed
a drop of oil into the keyhole, and once again inserted
his makeshift key. He jiggled this, turned it this way
and that. The bracelet gaped like a pair of lean jaws,
and fell from Shadburne's wrist.

"Bully for us!" Shadburne cried softly. "Now hold
out your hand."

The key worked again; and Clay, too, was free from
the irons. Shadburne threw the discarded shackles on
one of the cots. They stood still and watched the sentry
passing outside.

"Give him a count of forty, and then open up that
sash wide," directed Shadburne.

Clay muttered the numbers under his breath, and at
forty he pulled the sash back against the inner wall. He

fastened it there with a hook. Shadburne poked his head between the bars.

"Too tight a fit," he groaned.

"Come back inside," said Clay, and as his friend did so he closed the port again. "It looked near about wide enough to me," said Clay.

"Near about isn't enough," Shadburne objected gloomily.

"Listen, isn't there some soap in here?"

"Yes, over yonder on that shelf by the basin of water. Why?"

"If we took off our clothes and rubbed soap all over ourselves—"

Clay took the cake of soap from the shelf.

"It's a chance, and it's the only chance," Shadburne approved grimly. "Mighty cold out there for bare skins, but if you're game to try it, so am I."

⤐ 15 ⤐

Escape

Quickly Clay and Shadburne stripped off their clothes. Clay stood barefooted and shivering. He picked up his shoes and trousers, and made them into a bundle. Shadburne was pulling the port open and again he poked his head between the bars, then brought it back.

"Help me," he said, and Clay took hold of the desk. Together they carried it across the cabin and set it just below the port.

Shadburne put the cake of soap in the washbasin and vigorously stirred up a thick foamy lather. He smeared it upon himself with a liberal hand, not neglecting arms, legs, hair, or pointed beard. Clay followed suit. Finally Shadburne directed:

"Stand by to shove me through, and throw my pants and boots out after me. I'll make the try as soon as the sentry passes the next time. If I make it, you ought to be able to. I'll help drag you out."

They waited. Rain plopped along the rails, the deck. The tread of the sentry came to their ears, heavy and measured. The dark silhouette approached, passed between their port and the lanterns at the barge's side. Shadburne peered out to watch the man depart.

"Here goes," he said.

He put a knee on the desk, and began to writhe out sideways between the cramping bars. For a moment his body was wedged there, and Clay heard his panting grunts.

"Give me a push," Shadburne wheezed, and Clay caught him by his soapy feet and heaved powerfully, as though driving a battering ram at a door. One more moment of struggling effort, and out slid Shadburne head first. He landed with a muffled thud.

Clay quickly flung out Shadburne's boots and trousers, then his own. Between his teeth he clamped the faithful penknife that had belonged to Tryon. A moment later he was on the desk, squeezing his soapy head and shoulders out into the cold night.

Shadburne caught him powerfully under the armpits and dragged with desperate strength. As Clay kicked and struggled free of those clamping bars and landed on all fours on the deck, Shadburne caught up his clothes and made for the railing. Clay followed him, fighting not to gasp at the icy cold of the water. They stood in water almost up to their chins, holding their clothes above their heads. Rain fell upon them like the chilliest of baptisms. Almost at once, it seemed, the sentry was stamping along the deck they had left.

They stood still save for shivering, and listened until he passed on and beyond. Then, still holding their clothing out of the water, they waded side by side along under the overhang of the barge.

Beyond was the wharf, and Clay made for it, but Shadburne herded him away with the quick prod of an elbow. They slid between the barge's prow and the post to which it was moored, and came out beyond alongside a taller, bigger vessel.

"Come," quivered Shadburne, and Clay could hear his teeth chatter. They groped along the cold wet waterline of the ship. Shadburne wheezed in happy relief. Clay, floundering up behind him, found that Shadburne's hand was on a rowboat tied there.

They scrambled in and felt for the tethering line. Clay's heart sank when his hand grasped a chain, but Shadburne peered through the dark toward the boat's stern, then tugged Clay along with him. A second boat bobbed there, fastened this time with a rope. In they got, and Clay sawed away with the knife until the strands parted. Painfully careful, they shoved the boat clear and felt it drift into open water away from the barge and the ship.

They were both shuddering violently, like shirts flapping on a clothesline in a high wind; Clay wondered if his own agitation was from cold or from dread. Probably equal parts of both, he decided. Shadburne groped in the boat's bottom and found oars.

"Get dressed while I row," he said under his breath, and thankfully Clay thrust his icy-wet legs into the trousers. As he kicked one foot through, its toes knocked against something else in the boat's bottom. Stooping, Clay investigated.

"There's a knapsack and an overcoat here," he announced.

"I'm glad to hear it. We can use them in this weather."

Clay pulled on his shoes, then edged forward to relieve Shadburne at the oars. Both of them flinched sickly as something loomed darkly over them in the water, but it was only a buoy. Clay rowed downstream between the rows of ships on either hand, while Shadburne put on trousers and boots, then examined the things in the boat.

"Here, put on this overcoat," Shadburne told Clay.

"How about you?"

"Don't worry about me. There's a thick woolen shirt in this knapsack, and a blanket strapped on top of it."

Ship after ship towered gigantically past in the clouds of chilly dark rain. While Clay strove at the oars, Shadburne clung to the boat's tiller. Thus they traveled for perhaps five minutes. Then Shadburne called Clay back to steer while he rowed again. The rain buffeted Clay's face; but Shadburne, his back to the storm, pulled them powerfully along.

"We're past their docks and ships," said Clay at last.

"All right, steer us toward the south bank," directed Shadburne, shipping his oars.

Silent moments, while the boat glided toward the right. The bow struck something with a sharp grating sound, and their progress was abruptly stopped.

"We aren't stuck, are we?" asked Clay.

"No, there's a log poking out into the river here," Shadburne informed him, crawling toward the bow to investigate. "Come on, get out on the log while I hold fast. Take care you don't slip—this rain's freezing to the wood."

Clay scrambled out in the darkness upon a great prone trunk that flung out broken stubs of branches to serve as hand holds. Bracing himself, Clay grasped Shadburne's arm and helped him leave the boat, and they groped their way to the muddy shore. Almost as they did so, the rain ceased. They made their way among trees beyond the shore line, and then the clouds broke and half a moon gave them pale light.

"We can't stop here," insisted Shadburne. "They may know we've gone by now, and they'll be after us with guns and bayonets and shackles again."

"Which way?" demanded Clay. "Toward Petersburg? We can't be more than eight or ten miles from our own trenches."

"But the Federals have trenches between here and there, all of them full of blue-coated troops," Shadburne reminded him. "We head due south, and get to Blackwater Swamp and our own camp."

Clay felt his legs sagging beneath him. He had time to realize how weary he was, but there was no point in talking about it. They crossed a road, found a trail beyond, and moved along it.

"Take it easy, I see lights up ahead," said Shadburne at Clay's elbow. "Let's not run into any Yankee pickets if we can help it."

Stealthily they slid along between the trees for more long minutes. The moon hid behind clouds, and more rain fell. Now the glow of warm light was evident to the right. Shadburne stopped and tried to peer between the tree trunks.

"I'm going to climb this oak," he said. "Give me a boost up."

Clay made a stirrup of his hands. Shadburne put his muddy toe in it, sprang up to grab a branch, and swarmed up the oak like a raccoon. Almost at once he came tumbling down again.

"Yankees," he reported. "That whole part of the forest is strung with campfires. I saw lines of horses and parked guns."

"We can't be that close to their lines," objected Clay.

"We're that close to a mighty big bunch of them, and they aren't holding a position. They're just camped, on the way somewhere. I think it's that force we heard about, the one that cooked six days' rations and took a pontoon train across at City Point. Come on, let's pull out of here."

They made what haste they could, splashing through a clammy stream that drenched them to their shins, then wading in marshy mud. An hour went by, and another light showed through the wet leafless boughs ahead.

"More enemy," groaned Clay.

"No, there's a road up there, and I know it. I think that's the house of a man named Walsh. I made friends with him this last summer, he's been a big help to the Iron Scouts.

They sloshed across another stream, crossed the road, and came to a rickety fence before a little house with low eaves and a light in the front window. They listened, then Shadburne moved through the yard and knocked at the door. It was opened. Clay heard a cry of welcome.

"Come on in," Shadburne told him. "We're all right."

Walsh, a gray-haired little farmer, shook both their hands happily.

"I heard you were out scouting somewhere," he said. "Come into the kitchen, there's a friend of yours having some hot soup with me."

He opened a door at the back of the front room. Bob Dulin stood there, his big revolver gleaming in his lifted hand, a thumb pulling back the hammer.

"Oh," growled Dulin, "it's you two."

"Disappointed?" laughed Clay.

"A little bit. The woods seem full of Yankees tonight, and I sort of hoped I might add one or two to that score of one hundred I want to make before this war's over."

Walsh seated Shadburne and Clay at the kitchen table, and hastily dipped out bowls of steaming soup, filled with bits of meat and vegetables. Clay ate thankfully, and Walsh hung up the wet blue overcoat by the stove and brought him an old checked homespun coat to cover his wet body. Shadburne no sooner finished his bowlful than he stood up.

"Where's your horse, Bob?" he asked Dulin.

"Why, he's out back, in the shed."

"What sort of shape is he in?"

"Right good shape. Fresh and frisky."

"I'll borrow him," announced Shadburne. "And I'll take that revolver, too."

He picked it up from the table beside Dulin's hand and shoved it into the waistband of his trousers.

"I'm sorry, Clay, but I'll need that blue overcoat, too. See you all at camp before long."

He was gone out the back door before any of them could speak.

"Shoo!" exploded Bob Dulin. "Took my horse and my gun and your coat without even asking us if he could. And left us to wade back across Blackwater Swamp."

"I do call that cool," agreed Clay.

"No cooler than the weather's going to be," put in Walsh. "That rain's going to turn into sleet before dawn. You two had better sleep here tonight."

"We can't," said Dulin. "George Shadburne's borrowed our stuff to go out prowling somewhere, and he'll be looking for us in camp with some sort of work for all hands to do. Come on, Clay, the boys will want to hear all about how you happened to vanish up toward the Rappahannock and came back by way of the James."

Again the cold, wet night, the dark way through the dripping woods. At last they reached the dense thickets within which the Iron Scouts kept their snug little shelters and their guarded fires.

At once Clay was surrounded by his friends, all asking questions at the same time:

"Did you get back behind the Yankees?"

"How did you come back?"

"Where's George?"

"Yes, what happened to Shadburne?"

"Let me get dry socks," begged Clay, "and I'll tell you everything." He dived into the hut he shared with Hugh Scott, and emerged with socks in his hand. "Where's Jim Sloan? Jim, how's Cherokee?"

"Near about too fat from lack of exercise," Sloan told him. "Crawl out of that drowned old coat you're wearing and put on this blouse I stole out of a Federal bivouac. It fits you right well, you look as if you'd just enlisted up in Ohio or Indiana or some place like that."

A big square of tent cloth had been rigged up to shelter the fire from the downpour, and under this shelter crowded the Iron Scouts, smoking pipes and munching squares of corn dodger as they listened to the story of Clay's adventures.

He told everything as briefly as he could, but questions constantly interrupted him.

"So Tryon's still a going concern?" demanded Dulin. "We ought to have wiped him out last year, when we had the chance."

"Let Tryon alone, he's a Yankee jewel," replied Clay. "He wouldn't listen to some loose talk about hanging us for the crime of being Iron Scouts. He said that these impromptu hanging parties only start the same thing on the other side, and he doesn't like it. In fact, he acted right friendly and glad to see us, and I know he'll be sort of glad to hear we got away."

"No gladder than we'd be to have him a prisoner here," vowed Shake Harris. "I remember that he was a right clever fellow, the sort I'd like to have on our side. And what about this big bunch of blue boys that was headed across the river?"

"We didn't hang around to find out for sure," said Clay, "but we know there's a whole nation of them, figuring out to go on a picnic for six days at least."

"We know more than that now," boomed Shadburne's voice.

Everybody started and looked around. Shadburne was just beyond the circle of firelight, tying Dulin's horse under the shelter of an overhanging tree.

"What's up?" cried half a dozen voices.

"The Iron Scouts keep a sorry guard without me here, for one thing," Shadburne scolded, pushing close to the fire. "A Yank could have come right in and sat down among you without anybody knowing it."

"No Yank would be foolish enough to be out in weather like this," argued Sloan.

"That's just where you're wrong." Shadburne was dead serious. "I was at that camp we saw, Clay. I pretended to be a courier looking for returns of troops fit for duty. What I heard made my whiskers curl."

"Don't stop now to comb them out," besought the huge Barney Hennegan. "What are they up to?"

"There's a whole army corps—the Fifth—and a division of cavalry," said Shadburne. "They got at least thirty guns. And they're going to push twenty miles south, beyond our farthest defenses, and tear up the railroad between Petersburg and North Carolina. Maybe strike down past the state line."

Everybody had jumped up.

"What do we do?" Jud Prioleau stammered.

"We saddle and bridle and head for our cavalry," replied Shadburne. "That raid's got to be turned back before they cut off all our supplies from below the Virginia border."

❧ 16 ❧
Mount and Gallop

At General Hampton's quarters, Shadburne's report was quickly made and as quickly acted upon. Before dawn the big cavalry chief had ordered every man and horse that was fit for duty to muster for a march and a battle.

There were perhaps three thousand troopers, in a dozen shrunken regiments, and two shabby but ready-looking batteries of horse artillery. They did not seem like a tremendous host to Clay, who so lately had been looking at the hordes of Federals around City Point. As Hampton rode along the front row of his force on a quick inspection, the storm began again. But, Clay realized at once, the rain had frozen into sleet. Clay heard it rattle on the cold ground beside him as he stood with his hand on Cherokee's rein, close to the bit.

"Are you Clay Buckner?" asked a voice. It was a mail orderly, coming toward him. "Here's a letter addressed to you, care of headquarters."

Clay took the envelope and read his name on it. The handwriting was Lark Winstead's.

"Mount up, Iron Scouts," he heard Shadburne say, and quickly swung into the saddle. He thrust the envelope inside his pistol belt.

"Right by fours!" he heard Hampton's great booming voice.

"Right by fours!" echoed one regimental commander after another.

"March!"

The cavalry stirred into action, forming columns.

A courier trotted up to the Iron Scouts. "Sergeant Shadburne! General Hampton says for your command to report to him at the head of the march."

"Follow me," Shadburne called out, and the scouts moved after him. There were fourteen of them, under Dick Hogan and Bill Mikler. They moved briskly past regiment after regiment and caught up with Hampton, huge in his saddle.

"Sergeant Shadburne," said Hampton at once, "I want your men out ahead of the main body. Show us the quickest and shortest way to catch up with that raiding column of infantry."

"Yes, sir," answered Shadburne. "Where do you want to strike them?"

"Wherever and whenever we can find them," Hampton told him dryly. "We haven't anything like a tenth of their numbers, but if we make a bold demonstration it will slow them up, maybe stop them for a while. And that will give our Third Corps—A. P. Hill's men—a chance to cut through below here and head them off from the railroad."

"Forward, Iron Scouts!" yelled Shadburne. "Hogan, take your squad to the front. Mikler will follow, in closer formation. Where's Clay Buckner? Ride along with me, Clay."

The sleet battered their shoulders and hat brims, but the dull light of morning came grayly through the clouds. Clay tore open Lark's letter and bent above it as he rode.

Dear Clay,

I told your mother I would try to write all the news from down here in North Carolina. We still feel close to Richmond, because we're only a few miles from the Weldon Railroad. . . .

"I almost forgot," said Clay under his breath.

"Forgot what?" asked Shadburne.

"That Federal corps is hitting the Weldon Railroad at the North Carolina line. My folks live close to that point, and the Winsteads are with them—Lark and Miss Celie and Mrs. Winstead."

"Thunder, you're right," exclaimed Shadburne. "How would you like to move up into point position?"

"Whatever you say."

Clay jogged Cherokee's flank with his heel and quickened his pace to ride through Hogan's scouts, into the buffeting sleet ahead. Shadburne caught up, then someone else. It was General Calbraith Butler. Clay saw the sleet collecting frostily on Butler's mustache.

"If we live through this storm, we needn't be afraid of the Yankees," Butler said cheerfully. "You men are worse off than I am. You have two feet each to freeze, and I have only one."

He struck the butt of his silver-mounted riding whip against the neat riding boot that encased his artificial leg.

On they rode, an hour and then another. Cherokee bore Clay nobly, without indication of complaint at the cold journey. The road they traveled plunged between clumps of trees that sheltered them somewhat from the driving storm of ice. Clay glanced back. He saw the breath of men and horses behind him rise like steam.

He rode ahead of all the cavalry of the Army of Northern Virginia, looking for the enemy raiders; but he gave Cherokee his head for a moment and finished reading Lark's letter. She gave him bits of news—the health of the family, incidents about the neighbors, the condition of the stock. At the end:

It is quiet here, and beautiful at the end of autumn. Your father was encouraged by the bountiful crops, and he and your mother hope that the cold weather means the end of campaigning, and that you can come home on leave. I hope so, too. God bless you and keep you, Clay. Somehow I feel certain that you have a charmed life and will come through all dangers safe and well, to meet me again in happy times of peace.

From
LARK

Folding the letter, he slid it into an inside pocket. Shadburne rode up behind him, followed by Wade Hampton and Butler and two couriers.

"Look up ahead there," Shadburne said suddenly, and Clay saw a flash of metal in the dull light between the trees.

"Yankees," said Clay.

He and Shadburne trotted forward and looked. A crossroad made right angles to the way they traveled. Cavalry approached at a walk, perhaps twenty of them in open order. Farther away, across a cleared field, moved larger bodies of mounted men.

"It's their flanking force," decided Shadburne.

Quickly they returned to General Hampton, who nodded as they told what they had seen, then spoke to a courier.

"Back at a gallop, and bring up the first brigade. Butler, deploy them for a charge. We'll hit that flanking party hard, drive it back on the main body of their infantry. In this storm they'll have to stop. It will give General Hill a chance to get across their front."

Away hurried the messenger. Out from its sheath rasped the huge straight sword Hampton wore. Clay heard the sleet bombarding its keen-whetted blade. The Iron Scouts bunched around Shadburne, drawing their revolvers.

"Not a shot when we charge," warned Hampton sternly. "Let them find out about us when we're in among them. A complete surprise, and we'll get them

on the run. Wait until you're close to the Yankees before you start shooting."

Behind Butler came more men, fanning out into line
among the trees to either side. Clay seemed to hear
Lark's voice, and her words were the words of her letter: *Somehow I feel certain that you have a charmed
life and will come through all dangers safe and
well. . . .*

Suddenly he felt certain of the same thing.

The year's fighting had begun in February just like
this, with a ride through sleety cold to overtake and
turn back an overwhelming force of Federal raiders.
And he, Clay Buckner, had lived through that adventure. He had escaped perils and overcome obstacles all
through the months since. This new adventure would
not destroy him.

Hampton raised his sword on high.

"Charge them!" he thundered.